POSEIDON IS MINE

GODS AND MONSTERS

MILA YOUNG

Cover art by Cover Reveal Designs

ISBN: 978-1793037961

BOOKS BY MILA YOUNG

HAVEN REALM SERIES

Hunted (Little Red Riding Hood Retelling)

Charmed (Arabian Nights Retelling)

Cursed (Beauty and the Beast Retelling)

Claimed (Little Mermaid Retelling)

Entangled (Rapunzel Retelling)

Dark Reflections (Snow White Retelling)

WICKED HEAT SERIES

Wicked Heat #1

Wicked Heat #2

Wicked Heat #3

Guild of Shadows

Darkfire

More on the way…

GODS AND MONSTERS

BY MILA YOUNG

Apollo Is Mine
Poseidon Is Mine
Ares Is Mine
Hades Is Mine

POSEIDON IS MINE

"Elyse?" Poseidon asked and my head swam. My name on his lips was intoxicating. When he spoke, warmth filled my body. His voice was deep and velvety, and I felt it brush against my skin, every syllable filled with a sensuality that translated into something deep and dark and delicious inside of me.

CHAPTER 1

Elyse

Heracles swung a fist like a wrecking ball at me. I sensed the disturbance in the air a moment before he punched, missed, and I ducked. I spun around and kicked back, hitting him in the ribs before he had a chance to sidestep.

He stumbled backward with a grunt, and I cheered on the inside that I'd caught him off-guard.

"Better," he said, lifting his chin, a hint of admiration in his eyes at my move. "You're still a bit slow. You can be even faster."

"Come on, that was great." I squared my shoulders. Heracles rarely dished out compliments. He always pushed to get more out of each training session, but it came from a caring place.

"It really was, and I'm impressed," he said. "But you

can do more. You're so much stronger than before. With every death, you have new power. It's not just about exploring this additional ability, but about controlling it to the fullest."

I nodded, stepping back into my fighting stance. I'd do what it took to be as strong as possible and defeat Death, to stop him from taking any more innocents, but first I needed to train, then find out where the bastard had vanished to. Where was he anyway? Out there plotting how to kill more people or gaining strength with each passing day to take me down?

"Again," Heracles said.

I expected him to swing another fist at me. This time, though, he kicked me square in the chest so fast I didn't feel the pain at first. But I flew a couple of feet and landed on my back. I couldn't breathe, and I felt as if someone had shoved a plastic bag down my throat. A web-like pain shuddered through my chest, spreading outward, and I groaned. "Shit!"

"Come on. Get up." Heracles leaned over me, his golden-red hair falling over his shoulders.

I offered him a trembling hand, and he yanked me to my feet as I gasped for air.

"You good?" he asked, the bridge of his nose wrinkling with concern.

I nodded, still sucking in oxygen. I leaned forward with my hands on my knees, relearning how to breathe. "Are you trying to kill me?"

He huffed a long exhale. "You have to be ready for

anything that comes your way, Elyse. X isn't going to give you time to recover."

I shook my head and straightened up. Fire burned in my chest. "X isn't doing drills with me. You are."

"I'm training you to combat Death himself. This isn't the same as centaurs and griffins. This is a different ballgame. You died, so you're stronger, but you're not powerful enough. You have to battle smart."

"If I need to be stronger, why don't I just die another time?" I asked. The logic made sense to me. Zeus had given my family lineage additional lives while we fought godly creatures. I'd used up one already when Hades killed me, so I had three left. It had resulted in making me tougher, meaning with each death, I'd become a more powerful opponent for X. But at the back of my mind it also reminded me I was pushing closer to my last death, the one after which I wouldn't come back to life.

X had to be stopped. That was my role, right? Protect humans at any cost, even to my own detriment. My dad had drummed that into me as I'd grown up, so it always felt natural, except now I'd lost my first life, and uneasiness slithered through me.

Heracles stepped closer, his chiseled chest reaching my face. He looked down at me with cerulean-blue eyes, and when I met them, I remembered his father, Zeus. He'd visited me, demanding I remember I had to keep battling for the *good* cause. That he'd given me power and I couldn't give up because who else would look after the mortals?

"Don't you dare waste your lives. You hear me?" Heracles growled, leaning closer, his breath on my face, just as his father had thrown similar words at me. "You can only die two more times. After that, it's over for you. And you're the last Lowe still fighting. If you're done, it's over. Endless people will lose their lives before Zeus decides to stop Death and the monsters, or maybe my father will no longer bother with the human race. He created the Lowe power because he cared for mortals, but if you die, he might not do anything. He isn't the same god as when he first blessed your family."

I sighed and stepped away from him, not needing the entire world on my shoulders. "You don't have to get in my face, Herc. That speech would have worked fine two feet away."

"I'm serious," he said. "Don't fuck around with this."

"Jesus, okay, okay." I lifted my hands in defense. "I was just spit-balling."

"Don't."

Heracles turned around. He was serious about training. Since I'd died, it seemed like he was terrified it would happen again. But I knew what I was doing. This new power was a thrill—I hadn't ever felt this strong. Sure, I needed more control, but I wasn't nearly as bad off as Heracles thought.

"So, I heard Poseidon is in town." Heracles walked

the mats in the training room where he picked up his water bottle.

I joined him, grabbing mine and guzzling the refreshing water. "Yeah," I said, putting the bottle down, remembering when Poseidon had arrived just outside my place a few days before.

"No doubt he's cleaning up Hades's mess," Heracles added.

I didn't answer him. That "mess" included me. I'd gotten intimate with Hades. He'd gone down on me in a police academy and driven me insane with pleasure. The god of the Underworld was irresistible, and I hadn't been able to stop myself. I'd also gotten it on with Apollo. Something about Apollo was so fucking sexy, but it wasn't just that. He was also kind and caring, despite his biker image and his every-man-is-an-island attitude. And he'd gifted me a necklace with the essence of the moon. Just remembering the night he'd whisked me away to the French Alps warmed my insides. I wanted to spend more time with him, get to know him so much better. Or was I fooling myself having such emotions?

I wasn't going to get into that with Heracles. Yes, the guy was my mentor. He knew I was falling for Apollo, and even Hades, but I didn't want him to know how much they really affected me, as I wasn't in the mood for another lecture.

Zeus had appointed Heracles to train the Lowes in the art of supernatural warfare. My entire family had been selected by Zeus to look after humankind, and even though I was the only one left, Heracles had followed up on his responsibility and did a damn good job of preparing me for war.

It was a pity this conflict was against Hades's fantastic buddy, X, and I was still on the fence on how much influence Hades had in bringing Death to Earth. The Greek Grim Reaper was such a pleasure to deal with while he sucked up every soul he could find, consuming mortals' life force before their time. Not.

"Why did Poseidon feel the need to step in?" I asked.

"He always gets involved with his brothers' fights," Heracles responded. "He's in the center of the family drama, trying to stop everyone from snapping each other's necks."

"I thought petty fighting was a human thing."

Heracles shrugged. "The three of them can be pretty childish."

Zeus, Poseidon, and Hades were brothers. But Hades was bitter because he'd been tricked into being the god of the Underworld by Zeus and Poseidon.

"Have you seen Hades lately?" Heracles asked, cocking a brow.

I shook my head. He'd told me the gods viewed love differently, that being with more than one of them wasn't a big deal. It was to me because I'd started falling for Apollo, and even though Hades was a divine pain in my ass, I couldn't help but feel something when I saw him.

Not to mention the instant attraction I'd felt for Ares, which must have been a moment of weakness. One god in my life was bad enough, but having any kind of feelings for three was asking for trouble.

I couldn't pretend that all of this meant nothing. The whole situation had played on my mind for the past few days, ever since Poseidon floated down from the skies like a goddamn angel. When he'd arrived, he and Hades got into an argument, and I'd left them behind. I wouldn't get in the middle of the gods' drama. Ever since, I kept away from all of them, needing to focus on dealing with X. Yet the gods played on my mind endlessly.

"That's it for today," Heracles said. "I have another class in ten."

I smiled. Heracles had started giving other classes at the community training center. It was good for him to focus on something besides the Lowes. I knew he needed other outlets because he had so much free time since it was only me left. Once upon a time, there had been hordes of us. He'd had his hands full dealing with the family, and I recalled Dad had told me they invited him to parties and functions, though Heracles rarely attended. How did he feel about me being the only one left to fight the monsters? I was his last shot at this—and that had to mess with him after watching everyone he'd ever trained die multiple times. Sometimes, I caught him staring at me when he thought I wasn't looking, and I swore he had pity in his eyes.

He was forbidden from jumping in to help or he'd be ripped from Earth by Zeus and forced back into Olympus. It must have been hard for a hero like Heracles to stand back, considering he and Death had a past. Tales had been woven about Heracles having battled Death long ago to rescue the Greek princess Alcestis from the Underworld, but obligation now forced his hand. He'd once told me he feared losing his divine authority if he went against Zeus. So, he did the right thing and sat on the sidelines while I fought.

Heracles deserved to live a human-like life. It was what he'd chosen when he refused to live on Mount Olympus with the other gods. But he had no one here on Earth that I knew of —he wasn't always the sharing kind. Maybe he needed to get out more, make more friends.

"What'cha doing later tonight? Feel like Mexican?" I asked.

He shook his head instantly, as if that was out of the question, and glanced away when he responded. "Got plans tonight."

"Oh," was all I said, gaining myself an *it's-none-of-your-business* look. "Well, whoever it is, have fun."

He stiffened, and that response told me a secret definitely lurked somewhere in his personal life. Interesting.

"I'll call you for our next session," I said, throwing my training equipment into my bag and zipping up.

Heracles nodded and followed me outside into the

cool morning breeze. He poured water over his face from the bottle. It cascaded down his bronze skin, and I shook my head, willing to bet he drove the humans in his class wild with either lust or jealousy. Yet I couldn't help but wonder who he was meeting tonight.

When I climbed into my car, it was just after 7 A.M. Heracles and I had trained since sunrise so he could hold the early classes after he finished with me and I could have a normal day's work.

Catina wouldn't be at work yet, so I drove to her apartment for a quick hello. She was a human, fully immersed in normal life. We'd been friends for years, and I liked spending time with her. She was a reminder that life wasn't always crazy, and at times, I envied the lack of drama and danger in her life.

"I would never be able to exercise so early," Catina said when she opened the door.

She was still in her robe after a shower, but she'd already applied makeup. It looked like she wore the newest trend of golden glitter eyeshadow, which I'd seen at the stores. As a columnist at *Foundation* women's magazine, she was always on top of the latest fashion trends. "Or arrive at my friend's house before showering," she added, pulling up her nose. "No offense, but damn, you need a shower."

I laughed and made a kissy face in the air instead of hugging her. Catina shook her head as she drew back, and I followed her to her bedroom. She opened her closet to choose her outfit for the day, and I sat down on the bed.

"Am I seeing you at the office later?" she asked.

"Only tomorrow," I said. "I have to edit a few things first as I have another job that's paying really well."

I was a freelance photographer and did quite a bit of work for Catina's boss, Tina. The job was fun when Catina and I got to work together for the day. It made me feel normal. Fighting gods and mythical creatures was fun and all, but sometimes I wished I was more part of the human world.

"Then we'll have to gossip now," Catina said. "How's your Pretty Boy doing?" She came out of the closet with clothes and dropped the robe, standing in her underwear.

Which one? I thought, but I didn't ask out loud.

Catina must be referring to Apollo. She wasn't fully clued up on how I felt about Hades and what we had. Or didn't have. I wasn't ready to share my comfort level with multiple lovers.

"He's out of town for a while," I said.

After Apollo had taken me to the French Alps, I'd asked for a few days to clear my head and make sure everything I'd experienced as of late sunk in.

"Why?" She pulled on a pencil skirt and shrugged into a white blouse.

I didn't know how to answer. Apollo wasn't exactly out of town. He was also lying low while Poseidon was around. Apollo wasn't allowed to be in love with mortal women. I hadn't found out about this until Poseidon had arrived and Apollo freaked out. Apparently, Zeus forbade it. That Apollo had fallen for me was a hell of a compliment, but now he was worried Poseidon would tattle to his brother, resulting in Apollo being tossed into Olympus, never to return to Earth. And in all honesty, that thought stung because I was just getting to know him and I wanted more, not to have him vanish from my life.

Uncertainty pushed against me like an invisible gale, tightening around my chest at the notion. I had no control over the gods, so I hoped things would somehow work out.

Which was why I'd agreed to see him on the sly whenever we could make it happen. The bittersweet decision was sour on my mind, but I refused to let it get the better of me when I had enough trouble to deal with.

"He's traveling for work," I lied. What else could I have said?

"And you're still good?" Catina tucked in her buttoned blouse and shrugged into a matching blazer to complete her power dress suit.

I nodded.

"What about the other one?"

What could I say about Hades? Our relationship was love-hate in the purest sense of the term, and I still didn't understand what I felt for him.

She paused with one foot in a shoe. "You're not exclusive with your boytoy?"

I hated having these talks with her. The more men —gods—I had in my life, the harder it became to explain to her. She was a standard monogamous-relationship kinda gal, as far as I knew. And I wasn't, it seemed. How could I stick with just one god after what I'd experienced with two?

"Doesn't he mind?" Catina asked after I didn't answer. She pulled on the other shoe and studied her final image in the mirror, looking perfectly put-together as always.

"He doesn't," I said.

That wasn't entirely true, as I didn't know exactly how either god felt about the topic.

"It'll work itself out," I said.

"I hope so for your sake, my friend," Catina replied. "Boy trouble only gets worse before it shatters your heart. Anyway, I better get a wiggle on and go to work."

I nodded, and we walked to the front door together. She let me out and locked up behind us.

"I'll see you tomorrow," she said and we headed to our respective cars. Catina headed to work, ready to live a normal life. I drove to my apartment to shower and start work on the photography projects I needed to keep going to make a living. I'd always loved taking photos, so it was a dream to work in the field, though some weeks I wished it paid better. And finding a more secure job played on my mind. Though lately I doubted

I'd be able to fit it into my schedule. Plus, I'd been feeling more and more like my human side was fading away.

Since I'd died, it left me feeling disconnected from the human world in a way I couldn't quite explain. It was as if I were torn in two.

Maybe it was just because I'd been so involved with the gods, their passion and their issues, that I hadn't focused so much on the human aspect of my life.

That had to be it.

CHAPTER 2

Poseidon

Leaving the ocean behind and walking on dry land was like stepping out of the cool of the night into the scorching heat of the day. Without waxing poetic, I hated it. I'd been the god of the sea for a long time. I had a palace of gems and coral on the ocean floor. Peace. Everything I wanted.

But I spent more time than I liked at Mount Olympus, thanks to the other gods and their childish endeavors. Just when I thought I'd be able to head back home, to sleep for a century and live my life in tranquility, I found out my brothers were playing games again.

I was sick and tired of their shit. Most of the time, I felt like the older brother to both of them rather than the middle one.

Heracles came to Mount Olympus to plead with Zeus for help. He needed a god to help Elyse Lowe because Zeus still forbade him from getting involved, insisting his son was there to train Elyse, not battle alongside her. That had been part of his agreement for Heracles to live on Earth—train the Lowe family and nothing else. I was no fool. Such a decision must have killed the great hero, Heracles, but for generations, he kept his word and trained the family. Nothing more. If it were me, I doubt I'd have stayed so obedient for that long.

At first, I didn't care the little human woman needed help. She was the only one left of her kind still willing to fight the devils and dangers X sent to the surface. But I admired her for such tenacity, to fight for something she believed in, a real cause, so I stayed to see what exactly was going on. Everyone needed a potential ally.

Then I found out about the amount of trouble Hades had caused, and the only person who could get him back in line was yours truly.

I hated being the responsible one. Every time shit hit the fan, Zeus and Hades fought nonstop, bringing others into their quarrels until they became unmanageable. I learned a long time ago that if I stopped them early, it wouldn't escalate. And I supposed it stuck with me to always jump in and put out the fires.

Maybe it wouldn't have bothered me so much if Hades had kept his issues on land. But X had just *had* to come to the sea, and that was my domain. So, when X consumed half a dozen fishermen who hadn't been ready to die, he stepped on my toes. How dare he take those men and cross into my territory? I sensed their deaths like a spear to my heart, but I'd been too late to save them, and now it weighed on me. I fought to protect people who revered the ocean along with all the creatures of the sea: the nereids, the Hippocampus, Cetus, all of them. Keeping them safe was my job, along with offering them a haven in my realm. But I'd failed, and that killed me.

If X interfered with my world, Hades needed a backhand because he was connected to X. The two of them had always been linked. Hades wanted to wander into my backyard? He had to know this wasn't going to go away. My little brother was a pain in my ass on a good day, but he was pushing his limits now.

And this wasn't a good day.

I marched the tarred roads of the city of Chicago, the place some gods made their playground. Who knew why my kind loved this location so much? It was dark and dirty. Only little of the beauty from when the Earth had been created now remained. The mortals walked around with burdens as I'd never felt before. What could bring them such sorrow?

But despite the dreary lives the humans led, they didn't deserve to die before their time.

So, it was up to me to get between Zeus and Hades. Again. Before Hades did something stupid enough to piss Zeus off and we had another fight on our hands. If they fought again, I'd lose another couple of decades trying to find peace between them. Though knowing my luck, I'd somehow get caught up and suffer Zeus's wrath. Like the time Apollo and I tried to overthrow Zeus in one of Hera's schemes. As a result, we were stripped of our divine authority and sent to serve King Laomedon of Troy, where I ended up helping build the towering walls that surrounded the city.

A familiar sensation rose through me... the one where it felt as if all there was in my life was the battle between my brothers. When had I last taken care of myself? When had I last done something solely for my own pleasure?

Sometimes, I wanted to do something for me.

"What the fuck are you doing here?" Hades asked when he opened his door. The house I'd walked up to looked like it was two steps away from being condemned. It was all but falling apart, the lawn overgrown, spiderwebs hanging from the tree branches. But Hades stood before me in sweatpants and a black muscle shirt, sipping coffee from a cup as if he lived in a hotel.

I pushed past him and into the house.

Hades cursed under his breath, but what was he going to do? Send me away? He knew by now that I wouldn't leave until the problems were all fixed.

"I like what you've done with the place, getting the humans to leave you alone," I said, looking around. The inside was perfect, well decorated like any upper-class home around these parts—the humans classified everything. Had he stolen the furniture or bribed his way around? Maybe he'd just taken what belonged to the humans he'd killed.

I gritted my teeth. That thought annoyed me more.

"So, are you going to tell me why you're here this time or am I supposed to play twenty questions with you again?" Hades stood tall.

"Don't get cute," I said. "It's not going to help your cause."

"And what cause is that?" Hades shook his head and sat down on the armrest of his leather couch.

I wasn't in the mood for games. "Simple. Stop fucking with the humans and I'll go away."

He ran a hand through his dark hair. "That sounds like a good deal… if I *was* actually fucking with them."

I narrowed my gaze. "Are you denying it?"

"Yep," Hades said with a shrug.

I huffed, tired of these games. "I can't believe you. You're so full of shit. I could have been home, deep under my beautiful oceans. Instead, I'm on land trying to pick up after you because you can't behave for two seconds when I turn my back."

Hades groaned. "Stop, for the gods' sake. You're grating my tits, and I'm over your whining. No one wants you here, so go home."

I laughed bitterly. "Poor Hades, that your life should be so hard."

He jumped up and marched over to me, getting right up in my face.

"If you want to blame me for shit I actually did, fine. But don't throw around accusations when I kept my hands clean. You should be breathing down X's neck."

"X is your shadow," I growled, my rage spiking. "He doesn't act without your say-so."

"He does now." His voice wavered.

Fear?

"I don't keep X on a leash, contrary to what everyone thinks. How the hell should I know why he's sucking the life out of the humans? I can't control him."

Hades's denial? Spouting more crap, then. More useless denials. What utter shit. How many souls had been lost? They hadn't even ended up in the Underworld. It was a total abomination, going against the order created eons ago. All while Hades sat in his home, pretending to be a mortal.

"Don't bullshit me," I threatened.

"Look, as fun as it is to fuck with you, I'm serious about this. When do I ever hide it when I'm doing something heinous?"

True Hades usually rubbed it in our faces when he'd been particularly awful.

"I'm just here to do my own thing," he said. "To find myself, as it were, and I want to be left on my own."

I shook my head, refusing to fall for his attempt at gaining pity. "That Zen shit isn't going to fly with me."

"Whatever. I just want everyone to leave me alone.

What's wrong with that? You want the same thing—you said so earlier."

Where was this coming from? Hades never spoke like this. He'd call anyone who said things like that "a pussy." But he looked dead serious. Had something happened to him to make him change? The brother I knew flew off the handle, pushed my buttons, got physical. The complete opposite of the god in front of me.

"What about the human girl?" I asked, changing topics to see if I could get him to open up.

His gaze slid away from mine. "What human girl?"

"The Lowe girl. She was with you when I arrived the other day, remember? Why was she with you?"

Hades shrugged. "How can anyone explain why women are drawn to me?"

I took in a sharp breath, refusing to let my brother infuriate me with his games. "Come on, cut the crap. Are you stopping her from doing her job?" Was he distracting Elyse while X murdered innocents?

He met my eyes, his lips thinning. "I'm not all bad, you know," he said in a tone that made me wonder what the hell was wrong with him. Hades never sounded so defeated, like he cared what others thought. If I hadn't known my brother better, I'd have thought he sounded as if he had... feelings.

Fuck, didn't we all. I lost my wife, Amphitrite, when she left me long ago. It had stung like a bitch because I once loved her so much, but I'd moved on with my life eventually. What we had would always stay with me as a memory, but now I questioned if love existed or if it was a myth. A fantasy exaggerated by humans? I'd gotten over Amphitrite and survived.

I stared at Hades, who looked so distant. Was he sulking over splitting up with Persephone? He'd been madly in love with her, and I believed their relationship was the real thing. But when I discovered it was a spell, I'd worried about my brother and how he'd cope. Such a blow wasn't easy to bear. Maybe I ought to have contacted him earlier, talked to him about it, seen if he was all right? But I was too late with that too. I gritted my teeth, remembering all the time I'd wasted on creating peace when in fact it made me incompetent at what I ought to excel at: protecting others, being there for my family.

"If you want to prove you're not all bad, stop this ridiculous charade," I demanded, but I took a deep breath, needing to control my anger.

Zeus always said my temper would be my undoing. Like the time I'd quarreled with Minos, the king of Crete. He asked me to send him a bull for a sacrifice to a god, and I obliged, but instead of carrying out his original intent, the idiot decided to keep the animal for himself. I'd been so furious that he lied to me, I caused his wife to fall in love with the bull and she gave birth to the Minotaur. Yes, not my finest hour, but the lesson was that letting anger control me only made the situation worse. With a deep exhale, I unfurled my fists.

Hades sighed, his shoulders curling forward. "Whatever, Poseidon. Go lecture someone else."

"I want to know why you were with her," I said in a calm voice. "If you're not stopping her, what are you doing?"

Too many things didn't add up. From Hades living on Earth to him being with Elyse—a warrior blessed by Zeus—and to X being on the loose. Hades had a purpose for everything he did, so I didn't buy this bullshit.

"With no due respect," he said. "my life is none of your business."

Hades stood and slammed the empty cup on the coffee table before he walked past me to the front door, and opened it.

"Where are you going?" I asked.

"Out," he said, slamming the door behind him.

I stood alone in his house. Nothing had come of our conversation—again. Hades was a tough guy to talk to when things were fine between us. But let's face it, it hadn't been smooth with us for a long, long time. We'd argued for who-knew-how-many centuries, but I couldn't deny it'd be nice to have a brother by my side to share things for a change. Not fucking argue all the time.

The only thing worse than being kicked out of someone's home was that person checking out. I didn't want to stick around Hades's place when he wasn't with me. It was probably why he'd done it that way. It caused less of a fuss.

I thought about what he'd said. If he assumed Elyse was none of my business, then she was exactly my business. The only time Hades wanted me to back off was when something happened he didn't want me to know about.

When it involved a woman, though? It baffled me. Hades was not the guy to fall for anyone. After the run with Persephone, I doubted he ever wanted to think about love again. So, what was going on here?

I left the house and stood in the quiet street, wondering which way to go. Hades hadn't told me anything about the Lowe girl. When he acted like it was nothing, it was usually something, and I planned to find out.

And people were dying. It was her job to look after the humans, but she was the only one left of her family. I could only imagine how hard it was for her to make it all work when Hades was this difficult and X was on a rampage.

The Lowe family had been around since almost the beginning of time. They'd always been good at what they did, but I hadn't ever found out exactly what my brother Zeus had planned when he created them.

Or why. And that worried me, as everything Zeus did had a motive.

Maybe I should look Elyse up. I wanted to know who she was, what she was doing about X. If Zeus had sent help, it meant she'd been struggling. But she hadn't given up, and that was a good sign. If she had, there would be no one whose sole intention was to fight X. Most of us gods kept to ourselves and didn't pay attention to what befell humans. I'd spent too long dealing with shit on Mount Olympus to see the problems here, so maybe this was the time to make a change.

Elyse would be my next stop.

But first, I had to find a place to stay. Hades seemed settled here among the humans, as if he were planning on a prolonged visit. Apollo had scratched open a spot for himself, and word had it Heracles was the number one bachelor around town these days.

Gone were the days when the gods kept to themselves and watched the humans make love and war on Earth. There were no temples for us the way there used to be, no sacrifices that paid homage. And if I built such a house of Poseidon, I doubted anyone would worship me or care. Humans these days revered man-made things like phones, which was ridiculous. I'd watched them for years, as they ignored families and friends for those devices. Regardless, if we gods intended to mingle with our creations, we had to join them on Earth and walk around like them. Understand their world.

And if some of the other gods could integrate, I guess I could do the same for a while before returning home. Though I was curious why they'd descended to live amid the mortals.

I wasn't going to be here for long. I'd slap some sense into my brother, find out who Elyse Lowe was and how she'd stop X, and then I'd get the fuck out of Dodge.

I had an ocean to get back to, and I was already feeling a little dried out.

CHAPTER 3

Elyse

Messing around with the gods was complicated. And I hadn't seen Apollo for a few days, so not seeing him again played on my mind endlessly. I fingered the round glass ball on the necklace that was laying on the bedside table—Apollo's present. It held the essence from within the moon, he'd told me. A little something to help brighten the way for me when he wasn't around, but I couldn't wear it during training in case I lost or broke it. Plus, Heracles asked too many questions.

Apollo's gift still stunned me because I hadn't expected anything from him, let alone a present from his heart. I couldn't stop smiling each time I remembered him looping it around my neck, and the butterflies swept through my stomach once again. Gods, what was happening to me?

Yet my goal hadn't changed. I was still here to care for the humans who couldn't look out for themselves, and X was still running loose somewhere, hopefully not sucking the souls out of people and cutting their lives short when it wasn't time for them to go. Especially since I hadn't sensed him for days, so I'd focused on controlling my new power for when I tracked him down.

I had more strength than before—dying had been the best thing that could have happened to me.

It was sad I felt that way about losing a life, considering I'd cared so much for Hades when he'd killed me. But that ship had sailed. I couldn't afford to care for someone who could look me in the eye and shove a blade through my heart. As attracted as I was to him, I had to keep my head screwed on straight.

When I arrived home after a sunset run, sweat covered me, and my muscles ached. I pushed myself harder and further than ever before. My body needed to keep up with my new energy. Even though Zeus had imparted godly power to my family's bloodline, I was still trapped in a body that was mostly human and I had to be sure I stayed healthy.

I was about to strip and jump into the shower when a pulse shuddered through me. Electricity floated in the air, coating my flesh, and prickled on the back of my throat. It was familiar. Death.

A shiver rippled down my spine. The upside about dying—aside from the energy boost—was that I knew firsthand what dying felt like. And it wasn't a picnic. The darkness that had suffocated me still shrouded me now and then, submerging me for long enough that I worried I wouldn't escape the sensation—as if the world closed in around me with no way out.

When the fiery surge ran over my skin once again, I trembled. It was a lot more personal than a bat signal in the sky.

I had no doubt the pulses of power buzzing in my bones was X, so I hurried to my room and geared up. I couldn't sit home when he would kill more people. No matter how much he scared me. This was my mission, right? My plight in life, what I'd trained for, what Dad brought me up to do. He'd once called me Zeus's sword, to act on his behalf and protect humans. That was exactly what I'd do now. Not let him down or the innocents who didn't deserve to die before their time.

I had to fight with my new strength and that meant that my way of gaining an advantage had to change, so Heracles had ordered weapons for me. I still wore blades in the wrist sheaths to work with, and I preferred having my knife at my back. But Heracles and I were starting to practice using the Meteor or Flying Hammer, a thin metal chain with metal balls on each end I could flick as an extended punch, to trip someone up, or to deflect weapons. It was a lot more fun than the bo staff had been.

I owned a gun for the simple reason of attempting to work with the bullets to make them a better weapon against immortal creatures. Something my dad had been tinkering with, and I promised myself to continue his progress, though I hadn't made much advancement in that department. Besides, until I made headway with Dad's work, I couldn't afford to use guns when facing off gods as they could all disappear at will, and if I shot at X and he ghosted into thin air, gods knew where my bullets were going to end up. Guns worked for monsters that couldn't evaporate. Gods were ancient, and modern technology just didn't cut it, but my dad insisted someone told him the right bullet could destroy monsters. I hadn't figured out that right bullet yet. It might be a waste of time, but I loved working on the project because it made me feel as if Dad was near.

With my blades in place, I headed out again. My body hummed with my new ability, leaving me alert and ready to battle. With the adrenaline pumping through my system, I'd already recovered from my long run, and I didn't feel any of the usual exhaustion.

It didn't take me long to find X, and he glanced over his shoulder at me as if he'd been waiting for my arrival. Bastard. He was in an alley, and he'd cornered a bunch of kids. But I tensed as I laid eyes on X. Sweat drenched my skin, the throbbing of my pulse in my neck heightening. At once, a thundering surge of fire shot through my veins, a newfound anger. Encasing me, demanding I fight to the end, all rational thoughts vanishing. Only desperate hunger to fight X remained. To take him out. To end this. I recognized this influence he had over me, yet in my mind I battled between keeping sane and not rushing into combat. That was what he wanted, and how he called to me before, when Hades killed me.

X was sucking the soul out of one of the kids, the body turning into ash. What remained of the kid floated on the breeze, vanishing within moments. I curled my fingers into a fist, nails digging into the fleshy part of my palm.

The others were terrified, crying, whimpering, crouching in the corner. Their fear flooded my senses, bitter at the back of my throat. But the kids couldn't move—X had them trapped in a kind of spell that allowed them to see and feel everything but not escape. That was clear by their wide eyes, staying frozen on the spot when they could have run.

Knowing you were going to die and seeing it happen was horrifying.

"You're really starting to piss me off," I shouted, my muscles tense and ready.

X turned toward me slowly.

An icy ache dropped through me, and I twitched, fighting the impulse to recoil. He was scary as hell, but I couldn't afford to back down. His eyes were pools of fire, and somehow, I knew this was where all of his victims ended up. The flames fueled X, and he got stronger with each soul he devoured.

Newsflash: I was stronger.

I swallowed hard. Just because I had additional abilities didn't make it any less terrifying. It would have been so much easier if I could hide out at home, watch a bit of reality TV, and eat a microwave meal.

But this was my life. Seeing X consume these people was about as real as it got. And Dad's words about nothing being scarier than losing your mind to your own fear swept through my mind. Slowly, I took a deep breath and held my ground.

I had to stop X.

"You," he spat. The sound that came from his slit of a mouth was a cross between a raspy breath and a hiss, and I shivered as it slithered up against my skin.

"Yeah, I'm back," I said. "Wanna play?"

X moved toward me, and my resolve to fight him ebbed with each step. The spell broke. The barriers holding the kids dropped like an elastic band around my chest had snapped. They were free to go.

"Run!" I yelled at them.

But they didn't move—they were crippled by the all-too familiar fear.

"Get out of here," I cried out to them.

The first one snapped out of the daze, rubbing his eyes at first, and shot out of the alley. The rest followed suit—it only took one to break the ice and the rest would walk—or run—in his footsteps. I was glad they were out of the way. I knew how devastating terror could be, and X wouldn't hesitate to make them collateral damage if it came down to it.

I was scared too. I felt the same dread that emanated from X in a cold wind that had trapped them on the spot.

Instead, I reached deep down, grounding myself and gripping my newfound power with two metaphysical hands. I held on tight to the fire while unsheathing the blades on my wrists before throwing them.

Loaded with magic, they traveled through the air. The extra energy carried them with a whistling sound and they found X, tried and true.

One sliced his arm, and he hissed again. A red line appeared on his dark skin. His skin was almost the color of burned wood, his eyes like embers that would never go out, and around him, a fog of darkness canceled out the light, replacing it with something murky.

The other knife flew straight through him. He'd seen it coming and shifted his molecular density. It was unfair that he had extra tricks, but there wasn't much I could do about that.

At least he was distracted by my knives, which was what I'd been going for. Knives weren't going to take out this guy. I would have to do that. I darted forward, closing the distance so I was right in his face before he knew what was happening. I was so close, I could smell Death's shitty breath.

Bravery, my dad had once said, *was all I needed to*

defeat the enemy. And right now, I wore it as a straitjacket.

My body hummed, and I struck X twice on the jaw. He staggered back at my strength. A thrill traveled through me. I hadn't been able to cause this kind of damage before.

But he bounced back quickly and grabbed my throat. I tried to push magic into my skin as my body burned up, my flesh growing hot to the touch, but X had spent a life in hell. He didn't care about the scorching heat.

I'd underestimated him. Or overestimated myself.

Shit.

I was in trouble. My breathing cut off and I started to struggle. The more I panicked, the less grip I kept on my magic, and this was how he was going to get me. His amber eyes, the flames that plummeted into darkness, were right in front of my face. I squeezed mine shut. If I looked too deeply into his, I'd never stop falling. He'd roll my mind and spit me out, useless.

"That's enough!" someone shouted. The voice was deep and thunder crackled in the air. A moment later, rain poured. It started as a drizzle, but built very quickly, coming down harder and faster until we were drowning in a torrential downpour.

This was not normal.

A mini tsunami hit, soaking us through, and X let go of me. The waters kept crashing into me. I lost my footing and fell, my stomach climbing to my throat. It washed me a couple of feet down the alley before the water ran into storm drains. I coughed, pushing myself up and looking toward the source of the energy.

Poseidon stood in the middle of the rain, the water not ever touching him. In his hand, he held a trident of pure gold, which shimmered as he wielded it, lifting it over his head and bringing it down onto X.

X shrieked—the sound like all the screams of the humans he'd consumed combined, and I pressed my hands over my ears. The noise sliced down to the bone, grinding inside me.

Despite the terrible blow, X wasn't defeated. He struck back and Poseidon swung around. He wore a coat and it whipped around him, flying out like a cloak as he spun and landed a kick on X's sternum. The crack echoed in the air, and I cringed, knowing how that felt.

Still, X didn't go down.

"You can't stop me!" he screeched. He hadn't spoken much before.

"Yeah, but I'm going to have fun trying," Poseidon declared.

I jumped up and ran toward them. I'd help Poseidon fight. Two was always better than one.

I pulled the large sword from the sheath on my spine and charged X. My battle cry drew his attention to me and Poseidon lunged the trident forward, sinking the prongs into X's chest. His eyes flamed red at me, his mouth open in a snarl. He wrapped his black hands around the trident and made another noise that drowned out all others.

Then he disappeared. He ghosted away as if the battle had never been.

My ears rang after the awful sound, and I shook my head, trying to get rid of the noise. The earlier rage burning through me evaporated like steam. The same rage always hit me when I was near X. I hated that he had such influence over me, and maybe the training with Heracles ought to extend beyond the physical fight.

The rain stopped, the streets slick with oil after the water had washed over them. And I stood, trembling at how fast everything had just happened.

"Are you okay?" Poseidon asked, coming to me. His voice sounded a little distant, but my ears were recovering.

I nodded and looked up. I wanted to thank him, but my voice caught in my throat when he stopped before me. Last time I saw him, he got into an argument with Hades so fast, I walked away. I hadn't paid him much attention when I saw his anger. But now I had the time stare at him, I was lost.

Drop. Dead. Gorgeous. Shoulder-length wavy, black hair, a trimmed beard, and eyes the color of the ocean were only a start. His cheekbones were high, and he carried himself with the kind of authority that told you he could squash you if he wanted to. And he had the muscles to boot. The god in front of me oozed pure, raw power.

"Elyse?" Poseidon asked, and my head swam.

My name on his lips sounded intoxicating. When he spoke, warmth filled my body. His deep, velvety voice brushed against my skin, every syllable filled with a sensuality that translated into something deep and dark and delicious inside me.

How was this happening again? I couldn't seem to control myself around the gods. In their company, something took over me, an energy that called me to them. The opposite of the effect X had on me.

And fuck me, if this intensity was a direction toward someone like Poseidon, maybe I didn't want to back away.

"Where's X?" He glanced around, and before I could respond, he vanished into thin air.

I was alone, so I guessed that was my cue to leave?

CHAPTER 4

Elyse

The offices at the *Foundation* magazine building were light and bright with plants and ornaments and faux mohair rabbit throw blankets and pillows everywhere, making it obvious women ran this world. There was no reason for the place to be dull while they did their jobs. It was how Catina explained it to me when I'd walked into the women's world the first time.

And why not? I happened to agree. Even though I was completely out of my element.

My mom died young, and even when I moved out on my own, trivialities like ornaments and fluff never found their way into my life. I always had bigger things to worry about like gods and monsters and dying multiple times until my life was over.

It was why I enjoyed being at *Foundation* so much when I worked here. I liked the feeling of fussing about nothing much. I enjoyed how the women seemed to care about the small things that made them happy just because. There was something enviable about being able to care enough about what you wanted to make it happen, even if it wasn't what you needed. And each time I came into the office, I promised myself to go shopping at the local home deco store and buy a few things for my place to dress it up more.

"Hi there, can I help you?" A young woman with a braid and wearing glasses caught my attention as I strolled through the lobby. She sat behind the front desk, her eyes smiling, her posture stiff as if she'd practiced how to welcome people so long it now showed. I'd visited Foundation enough times to know she wasn't the regular receptionist.

"I'm Elyse and work freelance for Tina. She's expecting me. Is she in her office?"

She tapped something on her keyboard and glanced up. "Oh yes, she's got you in her diary."

I started to leave when she called me. "Sorry, miss, I forgot, you have to sign in the book. It's a new requirement."

I did as she asked, not wanting her to get in trouble. When I put the pen down, she stared at me, her hands in her lap. "It's my first day, and I'm so nervous."

"You're doing an excellent job." I smiled her way and headed through the lobby, past an open doorway into the main work area and made a beeline for Tina's office in the far corner.

After my meeting with Tina, the boss, I wove through the maze of cubicles in the large office space until I found Catina. She sat at her desk, a pink phone clutched to her ear. When she saw me, she grinned and waved me closer.

"I heard what you're saying, Martin, but I'm not interested," she said into the phone while she removed a stack of newspapers from the extra chair. I sat down and put my camera bag on the floor.

"I'll talk to Tina, but don't hold your breath… Yeah… Okay. Bye."

She replaced the phone in its equally pink cradle and sighed. "Some people just won't take *no* for an answer."

"It happens," I said. "You sound so serious on the phone."

She grinned. "I have to be. It's my job."

I looked around. In this pretty cubicle, I wasn't sure I would ever be able to be serious.

"So, how are things?" Catina asked.

Yesterday, when I'd stopped at her apartment, we'd barely gotten around to talking about the complicated stuff before she had to go. And it had been better that way. There was way too much going on in my life. The day had been so long, with so much fighting, it felt like a century ago already.

"They're okay." I nodded. "Tina is happy with my

work, so that means I'm getting a new job." Best we kept it to the trivial things.

"Of course she is. Your photos are fantastic. I don't know how you do it. You never look like you make time for your actual job and you still make magic happen."

Oh, if only Catina understood how true that statement was.

I shrugged. "I guess I'm just in the right place at the right time to shoot the photos."

Or rather, I fought the gods and their monsters, I trained, I went for runs, and after it all, I grabbed my camera out of my car and snapped a few shots that captured the essence of urban living. Something like that. I really hadn't focused nearly enough on my actual job lately, and I'd been lucky no one noticed. Some days I felt like a fraud for not trying harder. I was too busy fighting to keep everyone alive to concentrate on making a living.

"How is your man doing?" Catina asked.

Which one? But I didn't ask out loud. I pulled up my shoulders. "We haven't spoken in a couple of days. But we're good." I assumed she was asking about Apollo again.

"It doesn't worry you that he hasn't even called?"

I thought about it before I shook my head. I wasn't worried about what I felt for Apollo and what he felt for me at all. Somehow, I knew we were okay. Apollo seemed the who that fell hopelessly in love with someone. Fatally in love, had he been mortal. I didn't get the feeling he'd get over me in a snap. I wouldn't get over him just like that, either. Relationships with the gods were a whole different thing. And yet it was still something I was trying to understand. It became vital, like breathing.

Cliché as it sounded, it was the only way I could word it. And with Apollo, I needed all the air I could get. I'd never had any long-lasting, deep relationships before, so taking it nice and slow suited me.

"What about you?" I asked, turning the conversation onto Catina. "Anyone caught your eye lately?"

She shook her head. "No one serious. A few flings—you know me—but I don't think I'll ever find Mr. Right."

"I'm sure you will."

Catina believed in soulmates and that once-in-a-lifetime love that had never made sense to me. I'd seen it all around me, people who fell for one person and stuck it out with them for the rest of their life. My parents had been like that, too. When my mom died, my dad hadn't looked at another woman. Ever again. I couldn't think like that. It didn't make sense that there was only one love out there. Or maybe I didn't want to ever experience the agony I witnessed Dad go through after losing my mom to cancer. Him shutting out the world, spending days upon days locked up in his room, the life gone from his eyes. I cried for weeks for her to come back, but I'd been young and dealt with the loss quicker than Dad.

When it came to soulmates, what if you missed them? Took the wrong turn and your paths never crossed? What if you never found each other, were born in different countries or cultures or religions? What if you walked past each other every day and didn't know it, and you both ended up spending your lives alone?

Humans weren't meant to mate for life. Religion and culture forced us into that, but I believed we could fit with different people. I thought the kind of love Catina held on to only caged us. I wanted to be free.

"What about Oliver?" Catina asked me.

I sighed at hearing my neighbor's name. "What about him?"

Oliver had tried for so long to get a date with me. And then, when I felt like the gods had been driving me crazy and I'd be better off with a human, I had agreed to go out to dinner with him. A quick get-together to know each other better, but the evening never happened. Hades started his shit and Heracles came to fetch me. And Zeus turned up. Oliver had been more than intimidated, and I had ended up bailing on the poor guy.

I wasn't going down that road again. He'd never rev me up the way the gods did. He was a nice guy, but I'd only end up hurting him. I didn't want to do that to him, and he deserved to find someone who cared for him the way he would for her.

"He's just not my type, Cat," I said.

"He's so nice, though." Softness flooded her eyes and she stared at me as if she were describing an adorable puppy needing a home.

"So? Date him then." I nudged her shoulders and smirked.

She chuckled and shook her head. "It doesn't work that way."

Didn't it? Maybe not. I didn't know how it worked, though. From my experience, the gods approached me and I damn near melted into my panties right away. That was how it had turned out for me lately. But it didn't function like that for Catina.

"Miss Lowe?" a female voice asked.

Catina and I both turned. A timid-looking receptionist with glasses stood in front of us.

"Yeah?" Catina asked.

"You have a visitor," she said, staring at me, intently.

"Oh. Who's visiting me here?"

I stood to follow her to the lobby, where visitors were required to wait. And Poseidon appeared behind her, striding down past the cubicles, towering over her. The receptionist spun around and swallowed before looking my way. Her eyes were filled with stars, and I could understand why. Poseidon was a hunk out on the battlefield. In the office, surrounded by all the fluff and pink, he looked savagely male. Even in jeans and a black tee.

"What are you doing here?" I asked, my voice squeaking when it shouldn't have.

"I wanted to see you," Poseidon held his chin high, staring down at me.

I didn't bother to ask how he'd found me. I figured the divine power that coursed through my veins acted like a homing beacon to the gods. I wasn't sure if I loved that or hated the notion.

Catina looked at me with an expression of curiosity, her brow raised, suggesting she wanted to know everything. Stat. But I had to get Poseidon out of here. My reaction to him wasn't the kind of thing I wanted to do at my workplace.

"I can't talk now," I said.

"I won't be long." He stood as if nothing in the world could dislodge him. Behind him, several other women peeked out from behind their cubicles for a gawk at the hunk in their office.

I shook my head. "Long" was relative to the gods. A couple of decades wasn't long for them, either. Immortality fucked with your concept of time.

"Can it wait?"

Poseidon lips pinched at the corners of his sexy mouth. For someone with eternity on his hands, he looked pretty pissed about having to wait. The gods were used to getting what they wanted when they wanted, no questions asked.

I huffed. "Okay. Fine."

I turned around and picked up my camera bag, then gave Catina a quick hug. "See you later."

"Yeah, you will," Catina said to me with narrowed eyes.

She wanted to know what all of this was about, why yet another man was looking me up. And I didn't blame her. She'd never understand. But now was not the time to delve into the details of my love life or mission to save the world.

I left the cubicle and walked to the elevators with Poseidon falling into stride next to me. Everyone turned and watched us as we passed their cubicles. When I looked over my shoulder, one of the secretaries was following us back to the lobby, and I was pretty sure she was staring at Poseidon's ass.

My guess was it was a hell of a view.

The elevator was only big enough for the two of us, and the doors closed before the other woman could join us, as if Poseidon had willed them to. When we shuttled down, I was painfully aware of Poseidon. His presence filled the elevator, and he was so tall, his head nearly hit the ceiling.

"You can't just come here like this," I said.

"Excuse me?"

Right, a god didn't take orders. "The humans aren't used to you."

"I wasn't here for them."

Again. I straightened my posture and remembered

who I was dealing with and how general human behaviors didn't apply to him since he had no idea how to be anything but a god.

"Can we go somewhere to talk? Your place?" he asked.

I didn't put too much thought into his question and climbed into my car. Poseidon studied it with raised eyebrows before he doubled over and climbed into the passenger seat. He looked uncomfortable, his giant body squashed into the small space. I drove home with a grin.

It started to rain, and moments earlier there wasn't a cloud in the sky. Was the sudden change in weather a representation of Poseidon's mood? Still, my thoughts remained with him back in the office. I could only imagine how he appeared to anyone who looked at him. Tall, striding toward me with broad shoulders that could carry the world, and the cutest ass. He was fucking hot. For someone attempting to blend in with the humans, he was doing a terrible job. I bet every woman in that office would fantasize about him all day.

When we pulled up in front of my apartment building, Poseidon peeled himself out of the car, and we strode to my place together. Inside, he looked around, as though my way of life fascinated him, then gravitated to a framed image of the ocean I had on the wall. He reached out, almost touching the blue of the sea, his mouth pulling into a smile.

"Beautiful."

The image always calmed me and reminded me of the day I took the shot. My Dad had passed a few weeks earlier, and it was the first time I left my house in weeks, yet found myself drawn to the sea. No idea why, but I took a photo that captured that moment perfectly, and now it reminded me of my father as if he was with me always.

Poseidon moved to the framed photos on the television stand and fixed on the one with me and my mom. She had chestnut colored hair and mocha eyes like me. She was wearing her locket, engraved with a seashell. Inside the piece, there was a picture of me and Dad. Mom used to say when she wore the necklace, she felt as if we were always with her. But I pushed those memories aside, not wanting to get all emotional, and turned to Poseidon.

"Okay, we're here—alone. What did you want to talk about?" I grasped my hips.

"X," Poseidon said, taking a step closer to me. He took my breath away. It was hard to think about anything other than his body. His eyes were a tantalizing teal blue. I would drown in them if I weren't careful.

"What about him?" I asked in a breathy voice. With Poseidon this close, it was hard to draw air into my lungs.

Poseidon's eyes wandered over my features, his eyes

smiling as he took them in. He lifted his hand and tucked my hair behind my ear.

I shook my head and stepped back. "Don't do that," I said.

"What?"

"Don't touch me." I could barely contain myself.

Poseidon and all his manly glory stood right in front of me and so help me, all I could think about was sex. What was it about gods having such impact over me? Then again, thinking back to the way all the women in the office gawked at him, I doubted I'd be the only one struggling to push him away.

"I didn't mean to offend you," he said, his voice soft.

I shook my head. "You didn't. I just… can't." I swallowed hard. The sexual tension hung so thick in the air between us I could have reached out and grabbed it with my hands.

"Okay," Poseidon said. We looked at each other. Something shifted between us, fast and tempting, my pulse kicking into a sprint. I couldn't stop staring at his lips, and for those few moments, I thought, *Fuck it.* Why the hell was I fighting this so hard?

Two steps brought me up against him and his lips crashed down on mine. His hands combed through my hair, my arms around his waist, and his tongue slid between my lips. My body caught on fire. I wanted him so badly, it ached. He drove me back until we reached the couch and collapsed onto the cushions, hands furiously groping each other.

But this was just going to fuck me up even more. It wasn't that I didn't want this; I definitely did.

"No," I said, breaking the kiss as if I were coming up for air, gasping. "We can't do this." I was already in over my head when it came to the gods. I couldn't add Poseidon to the list of maybes where my heart was involved.

Poseidon looked at me with turbulent ocean eyes. "Are you sure?" he asked.

No, I wasn't sure at all. But I pushed my hands against his chest and he let up. If he hadn't, I wouldn't have fought him too hard. Thank the gods for small miracles.

"Yes, and you should leave," I insisted.

He stared at me, his eyes glazed over, confused. Had no one ever said no to him before? At first, I expected him to argue, but instead he turned and walked out the door, looking over his shoulder at me one last time. The bridge of his nose creased, and I couldn't tell if he was pissed or bewildered by me pushing him away. Was this why he came to see me?

CHAPTER 5

Poseidon

When I looked Elyse up, I'd intended to talk to her about everything going on with X and Hades. Get to the bottom of the trouble my brother had caused, fix it, and be on my way back to the sea to be calm for a change. I'd watch my fathered children from around the world, their successes, what they were doing, and let myself enjoy the essence of life. Even allow myself to believe that goodness existed in this world, because I'd been arguing with my brothers for too long, I'd forgotten how it felt to enjoy life again. Except now after X attacked Elyse, coupled with his insistence I couldn't stop him, I wanted to end him faster than anything else. To prove to the asshole he had no power over me.

I paced back and forth in the living room of a small

house I'd managed to secure on the outskirts of Chicago. Nothing like my underwater palace, but it would do for the time being. My intention was not to stay long. Or at least, it hadn't been before I'd seen Elyse. Now I wasn't so sure as other thoughts toiled in my mind about taking some time off for myself. Having some fun.

I'd meant to ask what Hades was doing to her—discover if my brother's bullshit was stopping her from doing her job as Zeus's warrior. I didn't believe Hades that he wasn't trying to make life difficult for Elyse. I wanted to hear it from her that he was a pain in everyone's ass.

But we hadn't gotten around to talking at all. First, there was the situation at her workplace. I knew the humans weren't used to living near gods, but they gawked at me as if I'd arrived from another planet. Perhaps I had—the modern humans hadn't been taught about the Greek gods nearly as much as they should have been. Somewhere along the line, their education had excluded who we were.

It was all ridiculous. I missed the days when we'd been feared and revered.

But seeing Elyse distracted me from the disappointment I'd felt when I walked among my people and they didn't recognize me. She was something else, and she made me feel alive again… something I'd forgotten for so long. I'd been with mortal women before, but none brought such a desire to enjoy life as she had. Or had

had such control over me. Perhaps Zeus's blessing on her family lineage that affected me so? Or something else?

When I arrived on Earth that first night and saw her with Hades, I didn't pay a lot of attention to her. I'd known there was something different about her, but Hades was my main concern. After I looked my brother in the eyes, I wondered if he was involved with Elyse. So locating her had become my next priority. But nothing prepared me for what I found when I finally looked her up.

I didn't know what Zeus had in mind when he bestowed his divine power on the Lowe bloodline, but Elyse took it to a new level. She was a fierce warrior. I could feel the determination, the stubbornness, the strength of will in her. The energy rippled across my flesh like getting caught outside in a spring rain.

And it made her spectacular. In all my centuries, I'd seen many beautiful women. Helen of Troy had been one of the most beautiful mortal women the gods ever laid their eyes on—so much so they became embroiled in the mortals' war. But Elyse was different. Her natural beauty, although it could inspire weakness, was nothing compared to the beauty of her soul.

But it was unadulterated lust that really crippled me when I'd been with Elyse. I desired her. I craved her all to myself in ways I'd never wanted anyone. Love had always been a sideline thing for me after breaking apart from Amphitrite. As much as I'd intended to spend an eternity with her, she had other plans with her forty-nine sisters, something about discovering herself, and that hadn't involved me apparently. Which was fine. It all happened so long ago, it sat on my mind like a distant memory.

Instead of talking to Elyse about everything that was going on, possibly offering my alliance, we'd slotted together as if we were pieces always destined to merge. I would have taken her—by the gods, I'd wanted to.

But she stopped me.

I hadn't planned to let go of the sexual tension that drove me wild, but the hypnotizing tone in Elyse's voice and the way she spoke made me obey her every word. When she pushed me aside, I had no choice but to do as she said. It felt as if she had a say over my existence in a way I wouldn't have thought possible. And that rocked me to the core. Usually, only Zeus held such sway over me. So why would he give Elyse such a power?

Someone knocked on my door.

I strode over and opened the door, expecting a lowly human who might have gotten lost. Instead, Hades stood before me, proud and his chin high.

"What brings you here, brother?" I asked in surprise. After our conversation at his house, I hadn't expected to see him again.

"Can a guy not visit his family once in a while?" Hades asked.

I straightened my shoulders and stepped to the side, letting him in. Hades strolled around, looking at the place I'd established.

"Living among the humans isn't so bad, is it?" he asked, and was that mirth in his tone?

"It will do for the time being," I said. "We were never made to reside so close to the mortals, but the situation demands it."

"What situation?" He twisted to face me, his expression intense.

What exactly was he doing here, anyway?

"Fuck, Hades," I said.

My brother was the only one who could get me to swear immediately. I didn't enjoy cussing. In my opinion, it was a weakness mortals had created as a conversational crutch. But Hades pissed me off, and I found using expletives the best way to express myself. "You think me being here is some kind of joke?"

Hades chuckled. "Nice language. I knew you'd embrace the ways of the humans. You had a pretty dirty mouth the last time I saw you, too."

"All the better to fit in," I said sarcastically.

Hades collapsed on the couch I'd placed in my living room as if he sat on his throne in the Underworld. I'd manifested some money and been shopping for a few things for my temporary home, refusing to live in an empty house while I stayed on Earth.

"This has to stop." I remained standing. This wasn't a social visit, and I wasn't going to get comfortable.

"What has to stop? You just got here. I'm not going to just leave you alone."

I shook my head. "You don't care about family. You never have."

"I resent that," Hades snarled. "I didn't banish myself from Mount Olympus or force myself to live in the Underworld. You and Zeus did that, remember?"

This was great. Hades was still bitter about drawing the short straw. And I admit Zeus and I had been assholes when we tricked my brother into making Hell his home. But that had been so long ago. You'd think a guy would drop a grudge.

"I'm talking about your business with X here on Earth," I said. "You're making things needlessly difficult."

He shook his head. "I told you, that's not my fault. I don't know what X has on his agenda, but I wasn't the one who put him up to it. Contrary to what you seem to believe, X and I don't sit down with an itinerary and decide how we're going to fuck up the world."

"Well, whatever you're doing, you're making life a hell of a lot harder for Elyse."

Hades narrowed his eyes at me. "What do you know about Elyse?"

"I know she deserves more than having to deal with X and all the bullshit you're forcing on her. You may think it's fine to ditch your job and fuck around, but Elyse is serious about what she's doing, and you're expecting her to save humans she won't be able to save.

How is she going to go up against X? He's stronger than he's ever been."

"How exactly do you know this?" Hades's tone sounded suspicious, and his arched eyebrow confirmed it.

"Did you think I could be on Earth and not have to deal with the motherfucker? He was climbing into Elyse, ready to claim her soul. Someone had to save her."

An expression crossed Hades's face too fast for me to read. He was so damn tight lipped about everything. I still couldn't figure out what his problem was.

"Elyse acts like everything is fine," I continued. "But don't think I haven't noticed what a struggle this has to be for her."

Hades suddenly looked angry, his brow furrowed, lips pinching tightly at the corners, eyes tossing daggers my way. "And I assume you know this much about her because you looked her up?"

"What did you expect me to do? If she has a job here, I can't very well let you ruin everything, can I?"

Hades stared at me, and I could feel his mind churning. I had no idea what he was trying to figure out.

"Oh, no," he said, his eyes widening a little bit. "Don't tell me you like her."

"What's not to like?"

One moment, Hades was sitting there, gaping at me. The next, he lunged at me with a cry that rattled my windows, and then he was on top of me, punching me in the face. I took a hit on the jaw and stars zipped in my vision for two seconds before I pulled myself together and retaliated. Hades wasn't going to attack me in my own home and win.

I pulled my trident into existence in my right hand and attacked him. His pitchfork appeared out of nowhere, too, and he blocked the blow. The sound of our weapons clashing was deafening. The room around us darkened. It was as if someone had drawn the curtains and snuffed out the light. I recognized Hades's anger filling the room. Well, I was right up there with him, rage sizzling under my skin. I had no idea why the fucker had attacked me, but his rage was contagious, and I brought a great amount of bitterness to add to the party all by myself.

"I can't believe it," Hades cried out while we fought. "You just never stop. It's never enough, is it?"

I blocked a blow to the head and elbowed him in the ribs when he got too close, recoiling behind me. He grunted but didn't relent, trying to stick the pitchfork in between my ribs from behind. Talk about a complete backstabber.

"What are you going on about?" I grunted.

"You and Zeus always take the good things and leave me with the scraps." He spun around and planted a well-aimed kick on my jaw. It sent me tumbling to the ground. Hades was on top of me in the blink of an eye, slugging me in the face. He straddled my chest, hitting me with a rhythm that seemed almost practiced. Through the bursts of pain and the ringing in my ears, Hades continued talking.

"It doesn't matter what I do. It doesn't matter that I did this shitty job you allocated to me better than anyone could, I will never be good enough. You will always come in here and take what you think you deserve without asking me how I feel."

Somehow, I squirmed out from underneath him and shoved him away. We stood a couple of feet apart, breathing hard. The metallic tang of blood coated inside of my mouth. It prickled my tongue. My face throbbed, and my head spun with confusion.

"I'm so sick of this shit," Hades said.

He leaned his hand on his knees, blood trickling from his lip. When gods fought each other, we could cause major damage. As immortals, we'd never be able to kill each other unless we had the weapons to do so, but we could do more than enough harm as it was.

"Stop being a baby, Hades," I said.

He nodded. "Right, I finally find something I'm serious about, something worth fighting for, and you call me a baby. It's so typical."

I frowned. "What are you talking about?"

Hades chuckled bitterly. "You're so good at taking what you want that you don't even realize when you do it. I shouldn't have come to Earth. I should have known nothing would have changed. But don't think you can do what you want with Elyse and not suffer consequences."

He shouldered me out of the way and stormed out of the house before I could say anything more. I was left behind, dazed, unsure what had just happened. Hades and I had gone from a conversation to a full-blown fight to nothing at all. And I had no idea why. What was he talking about? Doing what I wanted with Elyse? I thought about his reaction when I'd gone to see him first and asked about her. And now, the moment I'd spoken about her, he attacked me.

Could it be? Hades wasn't here to stop Elyse from doing her job.

No, the bastard had fallen for her.

Shit.

CHAPTER 6

Elyse

When I arrived home from my run on Friday afternoon, Catina sat on the steps in front of my apartment building, waiting for me. I smiled, loving that she'd come over for a chat, laugh, or whatever… anything to stop me from thinking about everything else in my life.

"I'm all sweaty," I said, approaching her as she stood up from the front step leading up to the building. "Not going to give you a hug."

"It's okay. I'm getting used to this." She laughed as she followed me into the apartment building and to my front door. When I unlocked it and let us in, I headed straight to the bedroom to have a shower while she put on the kettle in the kitchen. I adored that she was so comfortable in my apartment that she could continue without me for a moment—this was what real friendship should be like. We had to spend more time together, and I had to make time away from work, from training, from the gods. Just me and her taking a time out from it all.

I was in and out of the shower, and by the time I joined Catina in the kitchen, she'd already prepared two cups with instant coffee and she was about to take the kettle off the burner.

"Thank you. This is great," I said. "You should pop over more often if I get served coffee."

"Ha, who doesn't want a personal chef?" She giggled as she stirred in cream and sugar.

Back in my living room, we sat on the couch. I blew on the top of my coffee and sipped it tentatively. The hot liquid burned my tongue.

"Do you want to go out tonight?" she asked. "I haven't been out in a while, and I could do with letting my hair down. Need time to just relax, you know?"

"Yeah, I can do with a break too. It's been really rough lately," I said.

Saying it had been hard for me was an understatement. Recently, I'd fought more than ever before, and I was physically and emotionally drained. Not to mention all the different relationships and emotions around all of the gods I was involved with. And I still didn't understand my insatiable attraction to them.

"Is everything okay?" she asked, and she glanced at me over the rim of her cup, clear she was about to jump into inquisitor mode. Perhaps her visit wasn't just a friendly one but had come with a purpose.

"Yeah, I'm good. Think I just need some down time."

But she kept staring at me, unblinking as if she had something on her mind.

"Spit it out, Cat," I said. "What is it?"

She didn't pretend not to know what I was talking about and lowered her cup, her face serious. "Who was that guy who came to the office the other day?"

I'd known this would come at some point. I straightened my posture and shifted in my seat to face her. "He's just a friend," I replied.

"He didn't look like just a friend." Catina's voice lowered, as if we'd gone into gossip mode—like the times she'd told me about her work colleagues and who was sleeping with whom.

"How can you say that? He just came to the office to talk to me," I said.

She didn't know we'd kissed each other in my apartment after I brought Poseidon home. She didn't need to know, either. I wasn't even a hundred percent sure what was going on. There was no way I'd be able to explain it to myself, let alone to Catina.

"Look, lately, the guys in your life don't seem to be just friends. The only person with whom you are friends is Oliver, and he's the one person I think you should get to know better."

I shook my head, remembering my last conversation with Oliver making it clear we could never be anything more than friends. "I can't just date the guy because *you* think it's a good idea. You said it yourself: it doesn't work that way."

"So what, then?" Her brows arched. "You going to string along two, maybe three other guys? How does that work?"

I shook my head, fire toiling in my chest. I was getting irritated with this conversation, hating the interrogation when I hadn't worked it out myself.

"First of all," I said, and my voice came out cold, "what I do and whom I do it with is none of your business. We are friends, and that's great. I love sharing things with you, but you can't tell me what to do. Second of all, if I'm telling you that me and the guy visiting me at the office are just friends, I have no reason to lie to you."

The latter wasn't completely true. Lately, I'd been keeping things from Catina. She wouldn't understand how I felt—emotions and lust and all the other things were very different for the gods, and I didn't quite see myself as a part of the human race anymore. I was far from being a goddess, but I understood the way they functioned more than I understood how humans did things.

Catina's cheeks paled and she squared her shoulders in a defensive manner. "I just thought your morals were in a different place," she said, her lips pinching at the corners with the same kind of judgment Mrs.

Trotts from the corner store wore whenever I popped in there to pick up milk. She always asked me why I wasn't with a man, how young women these days were too frivolous. That store was off my list of places to visit for eternity, but the woman had pissed me off just as Catina was doing now.

I gripped my mug hard. "And who are you to challenge me on my morals?"

"I'm your friend. I don't want to see you hurt." She sipped her coffee, but her eyes never left mine.

"So then be my friend. If you want to be there for me and share your concern for me, that's wonderful. But you have absolutely no right to tell me what I can and can't do. Who said it was wrong to be attracted to more than one guy anyway?"

Her face reddened. "You are going to sink yourself, Elyse. You're in over your head, and before you know it, you're going to be chewed up and spat out."

Her words were like a punch to my chest, fueling the blaze that burned inside me. She had no idea what was going on in my life. Maybe I should have taken that into account, comparing what she was saying to the image she had in her mind of who I was. But I was too angry to think rationally.

My response burst past my lips. "Maybe it's better if you and I don't go out tonight. I wouldn't want my *immoral* life to get in your way."

"Fine," Catina snarled, standing up. She put her coffee cup on the table and marched to the front door.

I listened until I heard the door slam before I let out the breath I'd been holding and hugged myself, unsure what to do next.

I had no idea how to feel about this fight. Ever since I'd died, it seemed as if I was losing touch with the human side of my life. And now Catina and I had argued about something I couldn't possibly explain to her, it was all the more prominent.

My stomach churned with unease. I didn't want to lose my friend. Yet with X still on the loose, everything else in my life was trivial in comparison to stopping his killing spree, to save innocents from dying. And if that meant making sacrifices, maybe that was the cross I had to bear. But no matter how much I told myself that, my insides still crumbled.

"Are you okay, angel?" Apollo asked, stepping out of the shadows in my hallway.

I jumped around before I realized it was him, my heart pounding, and let out a shaky exhale as I shook my head. "Shit! Don't scare me like that. How long have you been there? Did you hear our conversation?" Heat curled up my neck and over my cheeks at the notion. Gods popped in and out of anywhere they liked, so who knew how long he'd been lingering in my apartment?

Apollo nodded. I didn't want to know how he felt about the fight I'd just had about having multiple men in my life. I couldn't take another argument. But Apollo was a god. He'd understand. Of all the people I knew, he was the one I needed right now. After how things had gone with Catina, I was so glad he'd snuck in here to pay me a visit.

"What can I do to make it better?" he asked with his seductive voice, taking my hand and interlinking our fingers. He was beyond handsome, built with so many muscles, his skin shimmering a bronze color as if he'd just been at the beach, and his golden hair reminded me of the sun.

I adored his touch and the tenderness of his voice. "Distract me," I said, gazing into his sky-blue eyes, letting myself fall under his charm. Something about his presence eased the knots in my muscles, reminded me he was here for me. Me! The person who was so messed up, I was losing my closest friend because I couldn't tell her the truth about who I was. I felt so out of control and didn't even know where to turn to next. Ever since Dad had been killed during battle, I thought my existence would consist of training and fighting. Saving innocents.

But now, I yearned for something more. A closeness to these gods, to see where this could go between us. And sure, a dozen problems about that fantasy hammered in my head, such as the gods living forever and I wouldn't. Except right now, I didn't care about any of that. I wanted to forget. To pretend I was so loved nothing could touch me, to fall into Apollo's arms and make him take me away from everything.

Apollo kissed me. Hard. His lips mashed against

mine and he ground his massive body against me, rubbing his erection against my crotch. He walked me over to the wall, pinning me in place. I'd missed this and been dreaming of him ever since our rendezvous in the French Alps. Now he was lying low, I didn't get to hang out with him as often and when things went wrong, I wanted to hang around with him, laugh, watch a movie, take the edge off. I craved a real relationship, and maybe such wishes were foolish. Especially with a god.

Except I had him now, and that was exactly what we were going to do. Lose ourselves in each other's company.

Apollo dipped his head and his mouth was on my neck, nibbling the skin. He pushed a large hand under my shirt and squeezed my breast, smoothing his thumb over my nipple until it was erect. I reached to his pants and undid them, pulling out his impressive cock and running my hand up and down the shaft. Apollo groaned. The sound of cloth ripping followed as he got rid of my shirt, not bothering to pull it over my head. I hadn't been wearing a bra and I was already half-naked.

Apollo reached behind him and grabbed the tank top he wore, pulling it off, evening the playing field. I ran my hands over his smooth back, feeling the muscles bunch as he curled his body around me. I was trapped between his thighs, small and delicate against his strong build.

His hands were sure when he pulled down my pants. When I was fully naked, he lifted me and carried me to the bedroom with such ease, I might have been floating. He laid me down and dove between my legs, closing his lips around my pussy. No hesitation. He'd missed me too. I moaned when his tongue pried open my pulsing, swollen lips. Tasting me, flicking, scoring me with his teeth. He sucked on my pussy's folds. The building ecstasy roared through me, my body melting under his, and my whole world was filled with him.

"Apollo, yes," I breathed, unable to stop my arching body, excitement claiming me.

He groaned and plunged deeper, his tongue finding every inch of my sex, his face between my thighs, devouring me. I felt the tightening at my center. He sucked so hard that I lost it. Completely and utterly. My core clenched and throbbed as the orgasm ripped right through me. It was amazing, and I screamed with pleasure.

Apollo moved up to my face and kissed me again. He was still wearing his jeans. I tried to push them down over his hips and ass, and he helped me. When he got them off, in two shakes, he'd wrapped himself with a rubber he'd grabbed from his pocket and winked my way. "Just to be safe and not get you pregnant."

My legs fell open for him. He climbed between my thighs and pushed into me. Fast and hard.

There was nothing gentle about the way he handled me. He slammed into me and fucked me, his hips pumping, and I cried out as the waves of ecstasy washed over me, erasing the fight with Catina, the questions about the damn war I couldn't seem to win, and everything in my life that just didn't make sense anymore.

This, I understood. This was right. Apollo lay on top of me, ramming his dick into my body, and I cried out and let myself go. He snaked an arm under my hips and lifted them higher, then thrusted into me deeper and harder. The slapping sound of our skin melded with my growing moans, and his groans. I didn't want him to stop, but to keep taking me for eternity. His eyes were on mine, but he was lost in the moment, in our pleasure.

Just as quick as the first time, a second orgasm drove me over the edge, and I came undone as Apollo continued to rock my body with his thrusting.

When I came down from my high, we were both breathing hard. Our bodies were slick with sweat and my skin burned with heat.

"My turn," I gasped and smiled.

Apollo grinned at me and rolled onto his back, holding onto me so we were joined at the hips.

When I was on top, straddling his hips, I was fully seated on him. I let out a deep moan and put my hands on his pectoral muscles. Finding my rhythm, I slid his cock in and out of me, riding him. His hands found my breasts and he squeezed my nipples. My heart beat so quickly. My clit rubbed against his pubic bone, my damp hair hung onto his chest and our eyes were locked as I fucked away everything that wasn't the two of us and what we were becoming to each other. A couple, a relationship, more.

I was sure Apollo could have carried on forever if he wanted to. He could hold out like no one I had seen before. But when I orgasmed another time, I cried out, "Finish with me!"

"Fuck, Elyse." And he did. He pumped into me, cock jerking as my body contracted and pleasure doubled me over onto his chest. When I lay on top of Apollo, breathing hard, his heart thundering in my ear, I let out a long breath.

"I missed you," I whispered.

"I missed you, too."

He stroked a hand in circles on my back. I listened to his heartbeat as it slowed down. We lay together as one, and I wished that this moment would never end, that I didn't have to get back to the war, to my complicated life. I rolled off Apollo and lay next to him, my head on his chest, and closed my eyes when a cool breeze washed through my hair.

I opened my eyes to find myself suddenly outside in a park beneath a huge oak tree in the middle of the night. Farther in front of us were dozens of people laying on the lawn, staring at an enormous outdoor cinema screen that played an old black-and-white movie.

Apollo, still lying alongside me, held me tightly and

kissed my brow. "A little getaway for both of us for a few hours to watch a movie. It should have just started."

"Where are we?" I glanced down to see we wore clothes, jeans and a tee, both of us lying on a fluffy blanket. Thank goodness we hadn't popped over here in the nude.

"Paris. The perfect setting for an outdoor cinema. You don't like it?"

I stared up into Apollo's blue eyes, the sincerity behind them, the admiration he held for me. "I love it. Never been to France before. The sudden change just caught me off-guard." I supposed I was still getting used to the whole being-swept-off-my-feet thing, and I couldn't deny that a girl could get used to this. Now, if only I could eliminate the other complications from my life, I could easily settle down with Apollo.

I laid my head against his chest as he held me closer, our bodies plastered together. "Thank you. It's exactly what I needed."

"Anything to make you smile, sweetheart." He rubbed my back in gentle strokes as we watched the French movie on the huge screen in the distance. While I didn't understand the language, I couldn't tell Apollo because I loved his gesture and all that mattered was that I was here with him.

I thought back to how we'd first met, how fast things had moved, and if this was the start of us getting to know each other better, I was ready to make it work.

"I would be just as happy staying in my bed with you for a week straight," I said, pressing up closer to him.

"Oh, that is easily done." He slid a bent finger under my chin and lifted my head to face him. "I've never felt so free around anyone," Apollo started. "It's easy for me to be around you. No drama or pettiness like in Mount Olympus."

"Is that why you don't want to return there?"

He didn't respond right away, but glanced up into the tree branches overhead, clearly the question was a touchy topic.

"If I go back, Zeus will find reasons for me to stay there. This is why I can't spend as much time with you as I want. I'll find a way to work around him forbidding me to fall for a mortal. You are mine, Elyse. I will destroy the sun itself if it means keeping you."

I smiled and shuffled up to reach his lips, not wanting him to eliminate the sun, of course. Yet I adored his dedication. "You aren't going anywhere," I said.

We kissed, his hand combing through my hair. Only now had it really sunk through me that being with Apollo was prohibited. He risked his freedom, and I'd lose the god slipping into my heart. Something constricted around my chest like barbed wire, but I couldn't let myself think that way. Not when so much was already out of control.

"So why is Zeus being an ass about you falling for a mortal? He created us. Does he not see us as worthy?"

"*You* are my equal." His voice deepened. "Not someone's toy to keep people entertained. So many of the gods see mortals as nothing more. But with Zeus, he probably thinks he's protecting me from getting hurt if I give my heart away to a human. I live forever after all, so yeah..."

His words trailed off, and I regretted asking more because this was the same fear smothering my thoughts. Each time I got closer to the gods, the trepidation of this not working out in the end hammered into me. I would die, and they'd continue to live for eternity.

So, I pivoted the conversation in a different direction because I doubted there was a solution to this, and I'd rather enjoy the moment. "What's it like in Mount Olympus?"

"Glorious and magical. It sits on top of the tallest mountain amid the clouds. Everything you could dream of can be found there, but the gods and their families are too busy trying to outdo each other to appreciate the beauty. They backstab each other. Get revenge for something or other. I suspect a lot has to do with boredom. But the longer I stayed there, the more I was drawn into the politics and exhausting games. Most nights, Zeus would order me to play music, chant poetry, to be their puppet. But I'd had enough, so I moved to Earth."

"To do what?" I asked.

"What all humans do. Find how to achieve endless happiness."

I had no response and cradled my head against him, embracing him. Apollo was no different to me or anyone who wanted to find themselves in this world. This universe. Just because he was a god didn't mean he'd found the perfect existence it seemed, and that made me smile. In a strange way, it made me feel secure about how fucked-up my life was.

"Do you miss it? Olympus, I mean. If Zeus and the others respected you?" I mean, sure, I was a bit more than a common mortal, but I couldn't compete with the gods and a paradise without sickness, poverty, and all the other woes we humans dealt with every day.

He kissed the top of my head. "I'm not going anywhere."

I closed my eyes and drank it all in. The beauty of our surroundings. The haunting memories of what he'd told me. The tenderness of his promise. I'd stay here with Apollo for as long as I could.

CHAPTER 7

Hades

You'd think that after a millennium of being the underdog, dealing with my shitty lot in life, and sacrificing my heart for a woman who didn't want it, I'd catch a break. But no, the hits just kept on rolling.

I had to admit, I hadn't seen this one coming. Zeus and Poseidon had always taken the good stuff, leaving me with scraps. But when I met Elyse, I'd thought this would be something I could keep to myself. Zeus and Poseidon had their worlds, the powers that obeyed them and the people who worshipped them.

That should have been enough for my brothers. Of course, I was an idiot. It was never enough for them to finish on top; they had to make sure I stayed at the bottom, too. Why was it so terrible for me to be ecstatic? Me being here on Earth had nothing to do with my brothers—they were more than happy in the ocean and on Mount Olympus respectively.

But Poseidon had come all this way just to take another thing I'd thought could be mine. And of course, he'd succeed. Everyone liked Poseidon better than me. Who had a moment to spare for the god of the Underworld? Who wanted to spend time with the person deemed to be the devil himself? They were all so sure about who I was, going with the stereotype and not finding out what really made me tick, that it was far easier to fall for my brothers.

And Poseidon was sickeningly perfect. He was a gentleman. He tried to keep his image golden, and every woman who crossed his path was more than willing to sacrifice herself to him.

I should have known Elyse would be the same. Although I thought she'd be different. I thought we'd had something special.

But I guessed it was hard to stay interested in the guy who'd killed you. I suppose she had a right to be upset with me and want nothing to do with me. Just like every other woman I'd ever tried to court. Including Persephone, who'd been cursed to be with me. If Eros's spell couldn't even keep that woman in my life, there was no hope for me.

I was too pissed off to feel sorry for myself. Wallowing in self-pity wasn't my style. Instead, I remained perpetually angry.

It wasn't just Poseidon who'd crossed me this time. Even though Elyse and I weren't necessarily on the best terms, it gave her no right to treat me like I meant nothing. Surely, the few moments we'd had together meant something? I wasn't willing to believe it was all for nothing—that this awful ache in my chest was one-sided.

I had to hear it from her mouth that she wasn't interested in me anymore, that Poseidon was better than me. It would kill me—I fucking hated that everyone's perception was my brothers were better than me, and I was doomed to walk in their shadows—but then, at least, I'd know the truth.

Elyse wasn't at her apartment. Not only did her magic call out to me and draw me like a magnet, it felt as if she pulsated inside my veins, a part of me I couldn't shake no matter how hard I tried. Even if I wanted to, which I didn't.

When I stretched out my energy into the universe, searching for her power in my mind, I found her at the training center. This was where Heracles prepared her for battle. Great. I didn't feel like facing my self-righteous nephew.

Except when I arrived, Elyse was alone. She was in the community hall, working with a weapon I hadn't seen her wield before. A Flying Hammer. In some cultures, it was a hell of a weapon when used right. And she was using it perfectly. I'd love to fight her, to see if she could hold her own with the balls and chain.

Something about battling her brought me to arousal, to see her fierceness, her strength.

Maybe we could get into it now. I was angry enough, and no one else was around.

I watched for a while from my shadowy corner as she ran through drills. Studying her was amazing. Her body looked taut and muscular, without an ounce of fat. Her dark hair was pulled back in a braid and her skin was shiny with sweat. Her chest rose and fell as she breathed hard from the exertion. No matter how many times she got it right, she did it again and again. This was how you mastered something—she seemed to understand that giving up, quitting, was never an option. Determination was sexy on her.

She set down her weapons, and I snapped out of my reverie. I was here to have it out with her, make myself forget the pity-party I'd held for myself, not to revel in her beauty. I stepped out of the shadows and into the training center.

She halted and turned to me, gasping and panting.

"What?" she asked. She wasn't in a good mood. Great. Neither was I.

"You're alone," I said.

Elyse nodded, her eyes narrowing in my direction. "It doesn't mean that I'm vulnerable."

"Oh, no. I am aware of that. You wanna tell me what's going on between you and Poseidon?"

She shook her head, her gaze falling from mine for a moment. "That's none of your business."

"So I just have to stand on the sidelines and watch you fuck whoever you want?"

Elyse raised her eyebrows. "Am I supposed to swear off all other men after being with you? You're good, Hades, but not that good."

She might have mocked me, but the way she stared at me wasn't a look of disgust, but appreciation.

I didn't think she was aware she was stroking my ego with that half-insult. I could show her exactly how good I could be. At the thought, my dick twitched in my pants and lust ignited inside me. But I was here to fight it out, not to beg for a body that would probably reject me, anyway. I needed to get the anger out of my system, to feel alive from the adrenaline combat brought.

"Why didn't you just shut me down? Why did you have to let me in?" My question surprised me as much as it stunned her, based on the way her eyes widened.

"Did you think I didn't want to push you away?" Her voice softened.

This conversation could go somewhere simple. We could talk about it like adults, I could tell her how I felt, we could come to an agreement or compromise. But I wasn't the type to be reasonable. I was angry with my brother, angry Persephone had never loved me, angry about everything.

I stepped closer to her, trying to intimidate her by getting in her face. "I think you take what you can get, and the more you can get, the better. It's my stupidity that led me to be collateral damage."

"Fuck you for saying that," Elyse snarled, but the emotions in her eyes were the opposite of anger. She was scared of getting hurt. "You want to treat me like a piece of ass, fine. I can deal with that. But don't act like I was the one who seduced you and then left you high and dry."

It was true. I *had* used my sexual prowess to reel Elyse in the first time. Sometimes, making women want me made me feel like I still had control over something. But that hadn't wound up being the case with Elyse. I hadn't been able to help myself. As soon as I'd seen her, I'd had to make her mine. She affected me like no other, and that terrified me—the idea I couldn't get her out of my head. I shouldn't be falling so hard for someone after all the shit I'd gone through with Persephone.

"Then what was it?" I demanded. "If you're going to run off with my brother, at least tell me that."

Elyse hesitated. And almost immediately, the atmosphere shifted, and that incredible attraction sparked between us again. This was what happened the first time. The lust I was unable to fight off, the feeling between us I couldn't shake whenever we were together.

I wanted her underneath me. I wanted her naked and stretched out. I wanted every inch of her body to belong to me. Elyse's eyes were dark, pupils dilated, and her lips parted. I sensed she felt exactly the same.

I didn't ask what she wanted. I didn't have to. Instead, I grabbed her wrist and spun her around. She started to fight back, doing what she'd been taught. She was stronger than she used to be, but my need to have her was stronger.

When she was pinned against me, face to face, I wrapped her braid around my other hand and tugged her head back, her slender neck exposed, her face tilted to me.

I kissed her hard, and she responded, opening her mouth, letting me taste her. She craved this as much as I needed her. I let go of her wrist and ran my hands over her chest, feeling her breasts, squeezing them roughly. She moaned into my mouth, and I inhaled her arousal. My cock sprung to life in my pants. She reached between us and gripped my cock through my jeans, biting my lip at the same time. I growled, something primal igniting inside me.

We were in the middle of the room, glass doors making us visible to the world. I had to take her away from prying eyes. I wasn't the exhibitionist type. So, I took her arm and pulled her with me deeper into the training center.

The next room was also meant for training, with mats on the floor and full-length mirrors along one entire wall. But the only window had blinds that were closed, and we were alone here. I kicked the door shut behind us and I was on her again in no time at all. I drove her into the corner next to the door and gripped her chin, pulling her lips to me. She wrapped her arms around me and grabbed my ass, squeezing. When I put my hands between her legs, she widened her stance to give me access. Her pussy was red hot through her pants.

I pulled the waistband of her training pants away and slid my hand into her panties. She was already dripping wet and moaned when I touched her. Her hands slid under my shirt and she dug her nails into my skin.

"Fuck," I bit out when she scratched me.

But I loved the sensation of the pain paired with our sexual tension. I was angry. I'd come here to fight. This wasn't fighting, but it was exactly what I desired.

Was it going to make things more complicated later?

Probably. Maybe because of the shit with my brother, too. But I didn't care about that—let him fight me for her if he wanted her so badly. I wasn't just going to roll over and show my belly.

I yanked her shirt up, groping at her bra. I didn't like how it strapped her in so tightly and I couldn't reach her nipples.

Elyse pushed against me, getting out of the corner. She climbed into my arms, wrapping her legs around my waist, and pressed her pussy against my dick. She groaned in my ear.

She clung to me, holding herself up with her arms and legs as I worked her shirt up. She removed one arm and then the other, and I dropped the garment on the floor.

When I laid her on the mat in the middle of the floor, I pulled her pants down, yanking her shoes off in the process. Elyse peeled my shirt off, too. We'd never gotten this naked before. It had to be skin on skin with her, nothing between us.

With my shirt off, I pressed my bare chest against her breasts and pushed a finger into her pussy, finger-fucking her while I kissed her. Her hands gripped my waistband, and I kissed her all over her face and neck as I rendered her useless. She was lost in pleasure, and this was how I liked her.

"Hades." She called my name in a moment of passion, her voice so fucking sexy.

I let go of her, only to undo my belt and my trousers. I worked them down my legs and kicked them off. A quickie with my pants around my ass wasn't good enough.

When we were both naked, I gripped my cock and guided it to her dripping sex. I wasn't going to go down on her, let her suck on me, do any of that delicious shit I dreamed about when I jacked off. I wanted her hard and fast and I shoved my cock into her. She was so fucking tight as I worked my way in, I groaned. She clasped my shoulders and cursed as I stretched her.

My hand slid to her throat. I didn't do anything

more than hold on to her, but it was so fucking hot, knowing she was in my control. But she wasn't the type of woman I would control. She was a free spirit and it was part of what made her so fantastic.

I bucked my hips, fucking her. I rode her harder and harder, pounding my dick into her, slapping sounds filling the empty room around us. My balls tightened, but I didn't want to come, not yet. Not for a while. I planned to take her long and hard, to eradicate all this fucking anger I was carrying with me. Half of it was because of her.

In a sudden outburst, her body convulsed beneath me. When she cried out, it was loud; she wasn't holding back. Her nails bit into my shoulders and her eyes were squeezed shut as she gasped in my ear, egging me on.

I sensed a second orgasm thrumming through her, or maybe three, before I pulled out. She trembled, her delicious body completely mine.

"Turn around," I demanded.

She opened her eyes, smiling with the sexiest expression. A simple nod, and she did as I asked. When she was on all fours, her perfect ass pointing at me, I shoved my cock into her again. Facing the mirrors, I looked up and met her eyes, which drowned in ecstacy. I winked at her and gripped her hips then fucked her from behind. She fell into another shuddering of arousal almost immediately and the pressure on my dick, my balls slapping against her pussy, was too much for me. I hadn't wanted to finish, but I couldn't hold back.

I cried out as I released inside her, and Elyse moaned, her body contracting, gripping my cock and milking it for all I had. I felt like the orgasm lasted forever.

When we finally slowed down, I was breathing hard. I pulled out of her, and she collapsed on the floor. She rolled onto her side and looked at me with hooded eyes.

I sat back on my heels, taking in the sight of her naked body. Then I reached for my clothes and dressed.

"Is this all it will ever be with you?" she asked. "Fighting and sex and nothing else?" She pushed up.

No, I wanted to say. I wanted it to be more, something we could hold on to even when we weren't fucking.

But that was dangerous. I was already too invested in her. And look how painful it'd already become. Doing more would end me, and seeing I was immortal, that was a very long time of pain.

"Yes," I said.

"And you're pissed off at me about it?" She sounded incredulous.

"I don't have to explain myself to you," I said.

"Don't give me that shit, Hades. You want to march in here and claim me, I get it. But don't get all primal about what I'm doing with my free time when you can't step up and make this shit happen between us."

I paused, stilled in the moment. She was right. But I couldn't afford to allow myself to feel all these emotions. I'd fall so desperately in love with her, I'd never get out the other end, the way I had with Persephone. And with so many other gods in the picture, Elyse was going to end up investing in someone else. Let's face it, women like Elyse just didn't build anything meaningful with a piece of shit like me. I was only good enough to guard the dead. They didn't even go anywhere, for Zeus's sake.

"I have to go," I said. "Get dressed."

"Don't tell me what to do," she snapped. Her defiance just made me want to kiss her again and go for another round. But I had to get out of here or I was in real danger of losing track of my emotions.

I stood and walked out of the room, leaving Elyse to scramble for her clothes alone.

Fuck, I was such a dick. But this was the only way I was going to survive without having my heart ripped to shreds again.

CHAPTER 8

Ares

Zeus had sent me to Earth to help the Lowe girl. To leave behind the war in the East, to come here, and straighten shit out. When he approached me, I'd assumed his request had been one big joke. I didn't care about these issues, and I sure as shit didn't want to get in Hades's way.

But helping out had meant I'd get to fight and that was all I cared about. Combat was all I wanted. I loved how I felt when I was fucking crap up. The adrenaline took the edge off, and it made me feel as if I was still good for something.

Because it wasn't as if the other gods, even though we were the same, liked me. I was the outcast among them. But they were wrong.

Ironic, if you asked me. Which no one did, by the

way. Why would they call me the weak one if I was the only one who would actually do something? I would fight anyone and anything, if asked.

Their accusations were such a crock.

And now? I was here on Earth and Elyse had told me to piss off. To be fair, she had been polite about it. Gods bless her soul. Elyse was actually a good one, as far as the humans went. Maybe it was because she had some divine power inside her or something that set her apart from the rest of the lowly mortals. Or that no mortal would dare speak to the god of War as she had. So, I had a soft spot for her.

Not to mention she was damn hot when she fought. I could tap that any day. But then, I was biased because I loved war. Either my name defined me, or I had earned my name, but I was who I was, and Elyse was a warrior, so she was a ten in my books.

That was if she'd actually wanted me around. Which apparently, she didn't. You couldn't ask for help and then complain about what you got. Which was exactly what she'd done. I just wasn't good enough for the job, apparently. She'd been so nice about it too. Saying it as if it weren't the insult it was. But I hadn't been fooled by a pretty smile and big doe eyes. She didn't want me, and I resented that.

What the hell was I supposed to do now? Wander around Earth and look for ways to spend my time? Sure, I could fuck around. I

D done a lot of that over the past millennia. But it

got repetitive after a while. Everything got dull after a while and I was tired of the rhythm of things, the way nothing ever changed. Though the notion of starting a war to keep myself entertained had crossed my mind.

Which would only piss off Zeus even more if I didn't follow his instructions first. Even if I wasn't wanted by the woman I was sent to help.

Go fucking figure.

Bitterness wasn't attractive on a man. Or a god. I was aware of that.

I wandered around the streets of Chicago, watching the humans go about their business. They were curious creatures, these mortals. Everything was such a fuss about nothing at all with them. They ran from one place to the next and worked themselves to death, only to repeat the same process again the next day. They seemed to have goals of some kind, but what was the point when they were all just going to die in the end?

That didn't make sense to me. If I knew I only had a few decades to live, I wouldn't create all these wants and needs. I would fuck around until I died. It seemed like the logical thing to do.

Hell, I wasn't even destined to die. Like, ever. And I was fucking around more than enough for all the humans combined.

Consider that my superpower.

When I wanted to, I moved around the city invisible to the human eye. It was how we gods visited our creations. And I did that now, following a couple of people when they interested me.

Currently, two teenagers caught my attention. They were dressed to impress in tight, short dresses—it was sweet how the mortals worked so hard to attract the opposite sex. Sexual attraction seemed to be a challenge to them. With gods, lust was prevalent. But the humans seemed to have to work at it. They didn't just drop their pants; they seemed to court each other. Win each other over with relationships, gifts, anything the other person desired.

I didn't get it. What was the point?

Right now, I was curious to see how it would work out for the girls, so I followed them for a while, listening to them talk.

"Do you think he's just leading me on, or do you think he's serious?" the blonde girl asked.

"You're going to have to ask him, but if you want to do that, you'll have to do it away from everyone. Guys are such asses when they're around their friends."

That statement confused me.

"Maybe," the blonde said. "I just don't want him to hurt me. I really like him, and if he doesn't feel the same, it might be better if I don't ask at all."

"But what if he does like you? He's so rich and super handsome. Then it will all be worth it, and you can date him. You'll be living the dream for the rest of us."

They giggled about it, but I didn't think it was funny. Love and courtship had never been anything I understood. Lust was all I needed, thank you very much.

Darkness drew my attention to the quiet street around me. No cars passed, but a few people bustled down the sidewalk. An itchy sensation crawled up my arms. Seeing that the Earth had become pretty damn grim since Apollo had decided to ditch his job, it was something to take note of when the Darkness made a statement.

A moment later, X appeared across the street. Tall and lean, he resembled a haunting silhouette with the longest black hair. He'd be invisible to humans too, unless he permitted them to see him.

I groaned at his presence, ignored the girls, and veered to the side, getting out of sight. It wasn't that I thought X was going to do something to me if he saw me. I intended to trail him and find out what the bastard was up to. What was Hades playing at with this shit? I couldn't figure out what he was trying to do.

X's dark gaze trailed the two girls I'd been tracking. He turned abruptly, crossed the road, and went after them. I stepped out into the street and followed him following them from a distance to avoid him detecting me. He was going to kill them. I could feel it in my bones.

For a second, I decided to do something about him. But Elyse had asked me to butt out, right?

X shadowed the girls until they turned down a side street. By the time I turned the corner, I found them farther down the empty lane. He had them pinned against the wall of a building, and the atmosphere reeked of their terror. The girls' souls poured out of their mouths and nostrils like fog while X inhaled it all in, consuming them. I was too late.

Disturbing fuck! This new thing he was doing—sucking the souls out of them rather than just taking their life force—was weird. The guy sent the souls to the Underworld so they could cross the River Styx with the ferryman, blah blah blah. He wasn't supposed to consume them.

X had inhaled it all, the soul, the body, clothes, jewelry…everything. What remained was a handful of dust that scattered on the wind. A shiver trailed up my spine. There was nothing left but the phone one of them had been holding, lying on the ground with a cracked screen. Perhaps he didn't like technology? What the fuck?

X shuddered, like the back spasm after a good piss, and kept going. Then he disappeared into thin air, and the earlier heavy energy he'd emitted vanished, replaced with the balmy warmth of the day. I didn't know what had made him suck up these two, but I felt for the families and friends they were leaving behind.

The parents of these kids would never know what happened. There would be no closure. X was hurting the humans in more ways than one with this weirdness.

Poor Hades. It had to be pretty shitty having this

guy as part of your identity. I'd never heard the guy complain, but to be fair, no one really listened to him anyway. Maybe he was pissed off about it all the time and no one cared to find out what his issues were.

Although, this was completely different than the connection between Hades and X I'd been aware of for so long. They just didn't seem as in touch with each other as they used to be. It had to suck ass to be joined at the hip with Death. But this was different. Hades wasn't even here to see this. Had he ordered X to behave this way? Though even as the god of the Underworld, this was low.

What if Hades just wasn't in on this? But that couldn't be. X wasn't supposed to be able to function on his own and make decisions without Hades and the Fates giving him the go-ahead. It was just how it worked. Everything was meant to balance out so everyone was happy.

Except those who died, obviously. But then, it was their time.

This? This was different. And it didn't make sense.

Where was Hades while all of this was happening? Maybe it was worth finding out.

I looked up at the skies. The sun was hidden behind a cloud of gray, leeching the color right out of life. The humans didn't seem to care too much. Didn't they miss the sunshine? They were attributing it all to pollution and global warming or some shit. Apollo had gotten off easy.

Hades. That was where I would get some answers, whether the bastard wanted to talk or not. I'd make him. I had nothing else on my agenda for the day, anyway.

Nothing else on my agenda for the next century. Perfect.

It wasn't hard to find Hades. The few gods who walked the Earth at the moment all had specific signatures, and Hades felt like a shitstorm waiting to happen. When I followed the sensation, I found him leaving a training center. The guy wore a grimace, pissed off about something—his anger hung on him like a second skin, and he tugged at his belt as if his dick bothered him. Except I'd witnessed his expression on countless soldiers getting it on before and after battles. So, who had he been with?

It wasn't too long before Elyse stepped out, and I smiled to myself. She looked just as furious. Her hair was a mess, and it wasn't her training that had made her look like this.

Hades and Elyse had gotten it on.

They were having a hell of a lot more fun than I was. I watched her get into her car and leave, curious what it would be like to have a woman like that by my side.

But if Hades had been here with Elyse while X had struck again, Death was definitely acting without Hades's say-so. The guy was all tied up in his head, probably not even aware it had all happened in the first place. The guy had feelings for Elyse—he tried to deny it, but he might as well have worn a neon sign around his neck because it was as clear as fucking daylight.

Something was up. Had Hades set X free? And if he was into the whole banging-humans shit, why was he letting X kill them? Or was he trying to rile Elyse up?

Nothing made sense. The only thing that did was that something was wrong. Which wasn't completely weird with Hades being in the picture. But still.

I intended to find out how this all stuck together. And seeing I had a whole lot of nothing planned for the next while, I might as well try to see what I could piece together.

Look at me go.

CHAPTER 9

Elyse

What was going on with me? I had no idea what I was doing. I'd gotten upset with Catina for challenging me on my morals and the number of guys I was getting involved with, but to be fair, I was in way over my head.

I'd never let her realize I thought she might be right. I was sinking a little each day as I feel my life going out to control, but I'd claw myself out of the hole I'd dug instead of admitting to Catina that I had no idea how to handle my mess.

I wished I could talk to her about my situation. I'd snapped at her and she'd left and now we weren't speaking to each other. Which meant there was no one I could talk to about what was going.

As a regular human, Catina wouldn't understand

what I was going through, and I had to change my stories up a little to talk to her about it at all. But at least she had been there for me, willing to listen, and she'd often given me advice that helped, even though she thought she was talking about something a little different.

Everyone needed a friend, even me. Even when I could bounce back from the dead a few times, I still had a heart, and it could still break, and I needed a support network.

Now, I had no one. I couldn't talk to Heracles about it because Hades and Poseidon were his uncles, and it felt weird chatting about my attraction to them. That was a total no-go.

I wished I could just call Catina and tell her I'd lied, that Poseidon wasn't just a friend, that I was crazy attracted to him, and I didn't know what to do about it. I wanted to be able to tell her my life was insane, and it was getting away from me. That all I yearned for was a break, to turn around and sleep a little, to sit and watch the sunset without getting ready for the fight the darkness would bring.

But that wasn't going to happen, was it? I wasn't a normal mortal, and even though I'd managed to have a friend for this long, I wasn't nearly human enough anymore. Somehow, dying had done that to me.

Losing a life was a bitch, I was starting to realize. But it had happened and now I had to deal with it. I'd always known I could die, that it would steal one of the lives I had here on Earth, so that eventually I'd end up dead for good.

I'd seen it happen often enough with the rest of my family.

But I'd never realized I'd lose my humanity, that the connection with the human world would die, too. And when I came back to life, my human connection would be so much weaker. Why hadn't Dad told me about this part? Had he been protecting me, or hoping I'd never have to face this? Well, if he was looking down on me now, what would he think? Would he be disappointed in how I handled X and the gods?

Sometimes, I felt like this whole bloodline shit with Zeus was nothing more than a curse. I'd lost so much, but what had I gained? And with X on the loose, what had it all even been for? From what I could tell, I was just continuing to lose.

And I was still nowhere when it came to Poseidon. With speaking to Catina and Heracles both out of the question, who else was left?

Not Hades, he was already pissed about Poseidon. Plus, after I had sex with him, I feared if I was in his company again, we'd end up doing something other than talking again. And I was still trying to sort out my feelings for him, and what the hell he meant to me.

Not Apollo because I wanted the few stolen moments I had with him to be more than whining about the rest of my life. And not Ares, because he was like a child who couldn't control himself with all his power. Plus, I doubted he'd understand.

Fuck.

That left Poseidon himself. I needed to find more friends and broaden my circle. Except all I could picture in my mind was his kiss, the passion, the hunger in his eyes when I pushed him away. He was a god in control and knew exactly what he wanted, while Hades's intensity was raw and animalistic. Apollo, on the other hand, brought a tenderness to his desire, but loved it rough, and that turned me the fuck on so much.

Maybe talking to Poseidon about what was going on between us wasn't such a bad idea. It did involve him, after all. And he seemed a lot more mature than his counterparts.

The more I thought about my decision, the more I liked the notion.

So, I went to look for the guy. It could be that I was walking right into trouble. If my reaction to the gods was anything to go by, I might be making things a lot more complicated for myself. But I had to try. I was driving myself crazy with my thoughts. He was a god and had to have answers.

Poseidon's energy was easy to track down as his tingling lure pulled me to him, and when I got closer and closer to where he'd holed up, the smell of the ocean rode on the wind as if I were at the coast.

I found him in a small house that looked as if it had

escaped from the seventies. Complete with a white picket fence. I half-expected an old cat lady to open the door when I knocked.

"Elyse," Poseidon said when he answered.

He wore jeans and a collared shirt with loafers rather than sneakers. He didn't strike me as a guy who could lounge around in his PJs all day. His black wavy hair was tied back into a short ponytail, and it made his handsome face only more striking.

He offered me a gentle smile, and I felt comfortable immediately, the panic leaving me. I'd been so nervous to speak to him and about what was happening.

"Hi," I said, both of us standing in the doorway.

"Are you okay?" He raised an eyebrow.

I thought about it and shook my head instead of nodding. "I don't know what's happening. I'm confused by what I felt with you. You're the only person I can ask right now."

Poseidon smiled again, wider, his eyes almost sparkling. Tingles swam in my stomach when he smiled. So far, I'd only seen two sides to him. Warm and gentle, yet also willing to fight for what was his or what was right.

And I admired that about him.

"I don't think it's a secret that I like you," he said. "But we don't have to do anything you're not comfortable with. And if you don't like me, too, that's fine. Then it is what it is." He shrugged as if he brushed off the emotions, except the haunting depth of his blue eyes screamed the opposite.

"You won't care?" I asked, trying to work him out, though in truth, part of me stiffened at hearing he'd be okay if I didn't like him. Who was this guy?

"Of course I will. But it's not up to me to decide how you feel."

I took a deep breath and let it out. "Everything is so complicated," I said. "I don't know what's going on with me anymore."

"I think you've been a bit too close to all the fighting and death for too long. You need to get away and just be who you are without all these pressures on you."

Poseidon was so normal about everything. So damn reasonable, I was almost suspicious. Somehow, I'd thought after what had happened between us, he'd be weird about it. I'd assumed this conversation would either end badly or we'd fuck.

But he was just a decent guy. And he was making a lot of sense, too. When had I last just had a bit of fun, letting my hair down and not worrying about the fate of the whole damn world?

"Let me take you somewhere," Poseidon suddenly said. "Away from here. When things get too much for me, I escape, even if just for a short time, to get away."

"That would be so amazing," I said, unsure what he had in mind, but I was ready to try anything if it meant clearing up my mind, the tangled emotions, the insatiability that curled deep in my chest for all the gods in my life.

He nodded and stepped out, closing the door behind him.

"Come," he said, holding out his hand.

I took it. His skin was warm, and his hand was big enough to envelop mine completely. He pulled me against him, and a thrill traveled through my body. "Hold on," he said, those ocean eyes deep when he looked down at me.

The earth quaked beneath my feet, and for a moment, my pulse raced as I suspected everything would collapse around me. But then we were on the coast, a forgotten shore with pebbles instead of sand.

"Where are we?" I asked, staring out at the beautiful calm blue sea, the endless curve of the beach where we were alone.

"Home. A place hidden from human eyes," Poseidon said, then inhaled deeply through his nose. The light breeze fluttered through his ponytail, and I couldn't stop looking at how incredibly handsome he was.

The sound of neighing drew my attention.

A jade and coral chariot stood in all its glory on the beach behind me, the wheels shimmering with silver and gold. Jewels adorned the edges with intricate leaves cut out of gemstones and fused with magic.

I gasped, convinced I was dreaming.

The chariot had four horses in front of it, but the

horses were in the water. It took me just a moment to realize they were not horses, but Hippocamps.

"Is that yours?" I said, my words rushing out. Silly me, of course it was. I'd heard about Poseidon's chariot and the Hippocamps that drew it.

Poseidon chuckled, drawing me closer by my hand.

I couldn't believe I'd thought they were horses at first. They had the heads and bodies of horses, but the manes were fins, and their front hooves were wide and soft like webs. Their hindquarters tapered into thick fins and they writhed and squirmed in the water, tugging at the reins, snapping at the bits in their mouths. Instead of coats, they were covered in scales that shimmered with greens and blues and golden streaks in the sun as they moved.

"They're beautiful," I said, in awe of these creatures, unable to stop studying them.

"They are." Poseidon helped me onto the chariot that offered enough standing room for both of us.

"Can I touch them?"

He nodded with a smile and patted the closest one. I leaned forward in the carriage, gingerly reaching out a hand. The closest animal was ever so still, as if knowing his master was there and trusted him. Smooth beneath my touch, the scales were silky with a slight stickiness, their bodies cold as if I touched a fish. I pulled back and couldn't stop smiling. I'd touched a mythological Hippocamp and locked the memory in my mind forever.

Poseidon picked the reins and clicked his tongue. The Hippocamps launched into the water, and I lurched backward from the sudden movement. Poseidon's arm was at my back, holding me closer, making me feel safe. The animals drawing us moved like fish, their heads and chests above the water as they ran or swam or whatever it was. The whole thing was like a dream. Oh hell, was this really happening?

The wind whipped my hair back and forth, the sea spray was salty on my tongue, and I felt every worry and fear fall off me, blown away by the breeze as we raced to the middle of the ocean, away from everything that could catch up with me.

When we finally came to a halt, the chariot floated in the sea. The Hippocamps splashed each other, neighing and bumping in the water, playing.

I laughed. "They are amazing."

When I looked up, Poseidon was staring at me with a smile on his face.

"What?" I asked.

"You're beautiful."

I blushed. Poseidon wasn't just gorgeous and masculine and everything a woman would want sexually. He was also kind and considerate, and I enjoyed spending time with him.

"I often come out here," he said. "Ride the sea, let myself think and enjoy the splendors. So how about you take control of the reins and take us for a trip around the waters?"

"You want me to steer the chariot? Will the Hippocamps even listen to me?"

Without a word, Poseidon pressed the leather straps into my hands. He clicked his tongue and we were off again. I squealed with delight and laughed out loud as we headed over the ocean. With a light tug to my right, the animals veered in that direction. Okay, not too much different from driving a car. And I put everything else in my mind aside and let myself beam with joy at riding a chariot across the freaking sea. No one would ever believe me, and as much as a selfie was a must right now, I somehow doubted anyone would believe this was real. Dolphins swam alongside us, and I had to be dreaming to experience this.

"If this was my place to escape," I said, "I'd never be stressed again."

Poseidon gave me a look as if he might say something, but he simply leaned a hip into the chariot and offered me a glorious grin.

"Dad once took me to Honolulu when I was young, and I felt the same way there. Relaxed and as if I could escape the world, even if only a few days," I said.

"There are some incredible beaches there."

I nodded and steered the chariot to the right, loving how the Hippocamps glided through the waters with such grace.

After an hour of me in control and Poseidon at my side, beaming with smiles, I had to get back to the real world.

I guided us back to the pebbled beach, though I doubted I did much, as the animals drew us alongside the beach as if well versed in parallel parking. Poseidon pulled me against him again and the Earth shuddered when he took us back to dark and dreary Chicago.

"Thank you for that," I said when we stood in front of his place again. "I needed it, and I'm now floating on clouds. You are very lucky to have that at your disposal."

"Any time," Poseidon said. "It doesn't just have to be about sex."

I didn't know how to respond, but my cheeks heated up. Our kiss back in my apartment had been me falling prey to my basic instincts, the desperate attraction to the god of the sea. But as with Apollo, our time together didn't always have to be about sex. Unlike whatever was going on with Hades and me.

I said my goodbye, and Poseidon leaned in, kissing me on the mouth, covering me in goosebumps. But when he pulled back, I did the same, showing him I had just as much self-control. I left it at that. Now I was even more interested to spend more time with him and get to know who he really was.

The city grew darker and darker as night fell. It hadn't felt like it was the whole day. When I climbed into my car, I fished for my camera. The sky, although very dark, had a spectacular combination of colors across it and I wanted to capture it. So I parked near the edge of the city.

When I climbed out of my car, I bumped into X, who appeared out of thin air.

He was dark and scary, and my mouth tasted like I'd eaten a mouthful of soil.

"Stay out of my way, girl," he said, bending over so his creepy face was right in front of mine. His eyes were pits of fire, and I tried not to look into them. But Apollo's necklace around my neck shone as if responding to X. He recoiled a few steps.

"If you don't, I'll end you." His voice was a mixture of a hiss and pure hatred. "But I'm also enjoying taunting you. Seeing you scared."

He disappeared as quickly as he'd appeared. I was suddenly hyperventilating, my fingers shaking. I nearly dropped my camera.

I threw the bag into my car again, jumped behind the wheel, and the terror urged me to speed to Heracles. I hadn't sensed X until he was in my face, and that terrified me.

"X came to me," I said when Heracles opened the door. He was wearing all black, as if he were trying to blend in with the shadows.

I was hysterical, my breaths racing, my voice taut, and I walked inside his home, pacing back and forth in his living room. "Said he'd kill me if I didn't back off. Is he actually declaring war against me?"

Heracles frowned. "That's weird."

"Your sympathy is amazing," I bit out.

Heracles shook his head, not caring I was having a

meltdown. I couldn't breathe. Getting caught off-guard scared me because that was how I could end up dead. I'd let the gods distract me to the point where I hadn't even detected X coming to me. And why was he suddenly now threatening me and not before?

"X doesn't talk to mortals. Not even half-mortals like you. He wouldn't stoop so low."

"Thanks," I said. My head swam, as though I was going to faint as I tried to process what had just happened. I rarely got caught off-guard, and I couldn't stop shaking. "But I tried to kill him before, so maybe he's coming for me in revenge?"

"You're a threat," Heracles said, nodding to himself. "That's what this is. He would never have challenged you if you weren't."

"You sound happy about it." My stomach twisted in on itself.

Heracles had always been there when I needed him, had always cared about me. My mouth was dried and I stared at him, waiting for him to say he worried about me.

Instead, he nodded again, folding his arms across his chest, and I was curious why he was so distracted and not acting himself tonight. "He sees you as a worthy opponent. Maybe your death wasn't such a bad thing."

I blinked at Heracles. What was going on with him? "Way to go on finding that silver lining, Herc. My life was just threatened."

Heracles sighed. "This is good, Elyse. He's scared of you."

I scrubbed my face with my hand. "It didn't seem that way. But if you say so."

"We need to do more training, so you're ready for him, though he won't attack you for a while, I'd say, since he just sent you a warning. We won't practice tonight—I've got to be somewhere." His gaze traveled to the sofa, where his coat draped over the arm.

I stared at him with narrowing eyes. "Where are you going?"

"Just out, but you're welcome to stay here. We can order pizza once I get back, and I'll keep you company?"

I sighed from pure frustration and fear locked around my chest. It was one thing to hunt down a fiend, but to know they were coming for me was a whole different ball game. He was Death! *Fuck.*

I turned to leave. "No, that's okay." All my weapons were back at home, and I knew my own place inside out. If any unwanted visitors turned up, I wanted to be on my own turf, sitting alone in Heracles's house made no sense and didn't make me any safer.

I clasped the round orb around my neck, the gift Apollo had given me, that seemed to repel X. "Thank you, Apollo," I mumbled to myself.

CHAPTER 10

Poseidon

"We need to talk." I pushed Hades's door open and marched into his house uninvited.

Hades sat on the couch with a device in his hands, staring at the television screen. He seemed to be playing a game of some kind, shooting humans with guns. It was very mortal.

"Hades," I snapped.

He groaned and paused movement on the screen before dropping what looked to be the controller.

"What?" Hades asked. "I'm playing Xbox."

"I see you can pause the game, so you can play later. So, you're killing people on that thing when X is out there doing it for real."

"Why are we back on this?" Hades growled, glaring my way.

I sat down on the wooden coffee table in front of him so he was forced to look at me. He leaned back against the couch like a sullen child and crossed his arms.

"Don't you care X is killing everyone?" I asked. "Why are you so indifferent about this?"

"What am I supposed to do? I can't stop him; I tried that. It's not my fault it's happening."

"If you're just sitting around playing games while he's out there killing, it looks a hell of a lot like he's doing your dirty work and you're okay with this."

Shadows darkened beneath his eyes. "Well, I'm not. Happy?"

"No." I raised my voice. "And this can't keep occurring. X is out of control."

"He's already out of control. This has nothing to do with me." He glanced past me to the paused TV screen.

I shook my head. Why was Hades acting so strange? He had to be involved somehow; otherwise, why brush it aside?

"What is it you really want?" I demanded. "Is this a giant temper tantrum? Are you trying to make a point? Because there are better ways to get us to listen than to kill off half the human population."

"You're exaggerating." Hades scoffed. "It's hardly half of the population. It's just a few here and there."

The burning fury in my gut coiled upward, but I bit

back my anger. "And it will become more as his strength grows. You know that."

Hades shrugged.

He really didn't give a shit, did he?

"Tell me what you want." I straightened my posture. "I'm here. I'm listening."

Hades barked a laugh. "Since when do you listen? Since when do you worry about me unless something goes wrong in your perfect little world? Don't act like you care now. All you're worried about is how this is going to affect Elyse." He huffed, the corner of his lip pulling up in a sneer. "But you should take that up with Zeus. He got her involved, not me."

He was impossible. That earlier anger shot through me like a terrible case of reflux.

"Killing humans is below you," I snarled.

"Yeah, it is. But I'm not the one doing it. X is. I've never wanted them dead. Not even the souls that come to me on time. Do you think I like knowing that they're going to swim in my river forever, not knowing who they were, so they aren't bothered about what becomes of them? It's sad, and I look at that crap every day. But it's my job, and all I give a fuck about is doing it well."

"But you're not doing anything at all now," I snapped. "Not your job and not stopping X."

"Because he's not my problem," Hades cried out, his lips twisting into a grimace.

"You unleashed him," I countered.

"I didn't." Hades sighed. "But if you're so fucking

worried, why don't you take it up with Zeus and do something about it? The two of you are much better at getting shit done than I am. You kicked me out to the Underworld, remember? Out of sight, out of mind. Don't make it look like you care about me now. You just need someone to take out the trash."

I rolled my eyes. We were back on that. Everything with Hades always returned to him getting stuck with the Underworld.

"Yeah, we fucked up," I admitted. "Is that what you want to hear? We were wrong to trick you. I know that. But I can't change it now. You're going to have to deal with the situation."

"I have been," he declared. "For the longest time, I accepted my fate. And that shitty curse Hera and Eros put on me to love Persephone, trying to get her to love me, too. I did it all. I played happy family. But it's not good enough. Not for you, not for Zeus. Not even for her."

I frowned. "I'm sorry about Persephone."

Hades responded bitterly. "She's just like the rest of you—you all think I'm nothing, and that will never change. I'm so fucking sick of your self-righteousness. All of you. But unlike you, who can fuck off out of my life, Persephone has to be in the Underworld six months of the year. And since she couldn't leave, I did."

He was so torn up about this. A throbbing pain settled in my chest at his heartache, and I'd played a hand in some of his pain by tricking him. We'd all had a good laugh when Hera cursed Hades to fall in love with Persephone. I'd never thought that it would rip him apart like this, and regret sat on my shoulders. I hated that I'd acted so childishly toward my own flesh and blood.

And there was Elyse, whom Hades had been so feral over. It was very unlike him. Because with Elyse, there'd been no curse to make him fall head over heels.

"Tell me about Elyse," I said, changing the topic so I could understand everything before I worked out how to fix this.

"Oh, fuck you, Poseidon," he sneered. "I don't need this from you. Not now. I can deal with my problems without your help, and you can't dig around in my head, either. This is my business, and I'd ask you to kindly stay the fuck out of it."

He was serious about her.

"You really care for her," I said. I wanted to hear him admit the truth.

He glared at me. His eyes were bright and filled with hatred. Hatred for me, I was sad to realize. Hatred for what we'd all done to him.

"Don't you fucking dare talk about who I love," Hades spat.

There was no reasoning with him, so I stood and towered over him. Pushing Hades would only end in us fighting again.

"Whatever your issue is, deal with it," I instructed. "If you don't want to talk, fine. But you have to get X under control and stop his killings. There are too many lives at stake here for you to have this shitty little fit about what you can and can't have in life."

Hades jumped up, anger radiating from him, and I prepared myself for another battle. He was serious about having it out, and I was angry enough I ached to fight him, too. I'd spent the day with Elyse yesterday and it had been great. She was a beautiful person, inside and out. And it was easy to fall for someone like her. A bright light in the darkest of times. I remembered her laughter as she'd guided my chariot, the way excitement lit up her face, and how much I'd yearned to take her into my arms and kiss her. To promise her the world and that nothing would ever harm her again.

I didn't want to see her hurt because Hades was being a pain in the ass.

Instead of attacking me, Hades sighed and plonked down again. He picked up the controller and unpaused the game, going on a killing spree. I watched for a moment until I realized he wasn't going to fight me. He hadn't walked off—he hadn't done anything other than get rid of me.

And I had no idea what to make of it. Hades was different than usual, and it was throwing me for a loop. What was I supposed to do with him? How was I meant to understand what he was trying to do with X?

I turned around and marched out of his house because there was no reason for me to stay if he wasn't going to talk to me. I could mull over his words somewhere else. And anywhere else would be minus all the gloomy vibes that came with Hades at the moment.

When I strolled away, I thought about X and how driven he was. As opposed to Hades, who didn't look like he cared at all.

And I wondered if something else was up.

X was an extension of Hades in a way. He was his own entity, yet they acted together. But this didn't make sense. X was acting on his own and Hades was missing-in-action.

Something was wrong. What if this predicament had something to do with Hades, not because he was consciously planning this, but if his bitterness was growing so serious that it was causing other things to go wrong?

If he could subconsciously sending X out to do things, we had more problems than I'd first realized. But to believe that was to think Hades himself was capable of mass destruction, and even though he was the god of the Underworld, keeper of souls, he wasn't the Destroyer. He was just my brother.

And I wasn't going to believe he would take the lives of so many innocent people. I couldn't. Even though there didn't seem to be any other answer.

CHAPTER 11

Elyse

I dreaded going into the office after the weekend. I had work to do at *Foundation*—I had to see Tina again to present my photos. I usually spent time with Catina when I went to the office if we worked on a similar project, but this time I dreaded seeing her.

My stomach churned after our last argument. I was doing the model shoots for one of her articles, and that meant being professional as we went through the photos together. Yet unease sat on my chest, speeding my breathing. I couldn't slip out of the building after seeing Tina and avoid Catina altogether.

"Hi," Catina said tightly when I arrived at her cubicle.

I unpacked my laptop. "Where can I set up?"

The tension lay thick between us while Catina opened a space on her desk and I fired up.

"How have you been?" I asked, trying to make small talk.

"Fine," Catina replied sharply.

And she didn't return the question.

We didn't talk about anything other than business after that. I worked through the portfolio I'd created for her, letting her decide which photos she wanted to use. The atmosphere grew more strained between us, and as soon as we were done, I packed up and left. If everything had been fine with us, we'd have spent hours in her office, pretending we were still working while actually gossiping.

It was sad. I didn't want to lose my friend, the part of me that reminded me I was human, that life could be normal. Someone who asked me how my day was, who randomly popped over with chocolate or just to make me a cup of coffee, then gossip about the latest drama at work.

I rode the elevator down to the lobby, feeling like shit. Was this the end of our friendship? I hated that it could be over. We'd come such a long way, but I had no idea how to fix us. Catina had overstepped her bounds by challenging me on my morals and questioning the way I lived my life. In all the years we'd been friends, that was the one thing we never did to each other. Then again, our lives had always run. Maybe I'd been fooling myself, believing I could keep so many secrets from her and not think it would somehow backfire on me.

Yes, so I had this hidden life no one knew about. I had magic and strength that wasn't human. But there'd still been a very big part of me that related to Catina and her normal life. Something I craved. I lived a simple life vicariously through her.

But it looked like that was all over. Since I died at the hands of Hades, everything became different. I hated how that included my friendship. I climbed into my car and drove home—there was nowhere else for me to go. Today, I was going to have to work through my issues alone. Get to a place where I accepted my situation, remembered why my father would always tell me not to get close to anyone.

You can't keep friends in this business, he'd say.

I never understood that because for years I'd balanced everything perfectly. But that was before the gods and X entered my life.

Usually, when I was in a bad mood like this, unsure about how to figure out my difficulties, a workout helped. But I felt as if I'd hit a wall with how much training I could do alone—there were only so many times I could run through the drills with the Dragon Punch before I got bored. I didn't want to go for a run; it allowed me too much time to think.

And Heracles was too busy with who-knew-what to train with me.

I was happy for him. He deserved to have a full life.

His sole purpose had always been to train the Lowe family. It'd been the only thing that kept him going. But lately, he'd started to develop other wants and create new goals for himself.

Though, part of me didn't understand why he was so secretive about what he was doing. Was it a new relationship and he didn't want to tell me in case it didn't work out? Hell, had he seen my love life recently? No way was his dating life as messed up as mine.

Not only was Heracles involved with almost all the classes at the community center, but he'd also started training the private students in the Asian art of fighting. I wasn't sure why this was one of his fortés, but he was revered by his students.

Besides, I doubted he wanted to put up with the gossip and drama. I might not have been like the rest of the humans, but I was a very far throw from the rest of the gods, and my issues were petty at best.

So, alone at home was the only option.

I carried my camera and laptop bag inside and collapsed on the couch. I switched on the television and clicked through the channels, trying to find something to capture my attention. But nothing interested me. Television didn't make up for the loss of a best friend.

Someone knocked on my door, and I jumped up. What if it was Catina? I hoped she'd come to talk, that she felt bad we weren't on good terms right now. I missed my friend.

When I yanked the door open, Oliver stood in front of me. He looked a little sheepish, and I deflated.

"I couldn't help but notice you were home," he said. "Do you want some company?"

I hesitated a moment before nodding and letting him in. We hadn't been spending time together. As his next-door neighbor, I bumped into him from time to time, but after our one attempt at a date and how I'd stood him up thanks to Zeus, he'd stay away from me a little.

I didn't blame him.

"Can I get you something to drink?" I asked. "I have soda in the fridge."

"Yeah, thanks." Oliver sat on the couch like the last time he'd been over.

When I had told him we could never be anything more than friends. When he'd gotten upset with me. When I hated being forced to push him away because I wasn't interested in him in the way he wanted me to be.

I retrieved two cans and walked back to the living room, then handed Oliver one. My can hissed when I pulled the tab, and the first sip bubbled down my throat.

"So, how have you been?" Oliver asked.

I shifted in my seat, unable to get comfortable,

unsure I wanted to answer that question. "I've been better. You?"

"Did you and Catina have a fight?" he asked without answering my question.

I looked at Oliver with a frown. "How did you know?" I hoped Catina hadn't said anything to him. She loved to gossip, but he was my neighbor.

"I saw her storming out of here, angry as anything. I put two and two together." He stared at me, his expression softening, as if he were ready to apologize for my loss, maybe reach over and hug me, but he didn't.

I shrugged and took another drink. "We just don't see eye to eye about everything. It's stupid that it's affecting our friendship. But we'll probably get over it."

I prayed that was the case and held on to the hope we'd make up. Losing a best friend was like having my arm chopped off.

"I'm sorry you're going through a tough time," Oliver said. "You know, I'm here to talk to if you need someone to listen."

"Thanks, Oliver," I said.

He was nice, but he was still hopeful something would happen between us. He wasn't as verbal about it as he'd been before—being turned down the way I'd done it must have bruised his ego. But I had to commend him for his determination. If I really were captivated by him, it would've been a good trait for a relationship.

"You wanna to talk about it?" Oliver asked when I didn't say anything for a while.

I shook my head. The truth was, I would have loved to cry on Oliver's shoulder about Catina. I desperately wanted to talk to someone. But I couldn't explain to him why we'd been fighting without detailing what had been happening with all the men in my life—as far as what Catina had noticed—after all. It just wouldn't go over very well with Oliver, the man still interested in me, to bring up the three different guys I was involved with. And I doubted he'd see past that to offer me the kind of support I sought.

Eventually, after Oliver and I made small talk, and it was clear I wasn't willing to go into the deep stuff, he headed back to his apartment. Maybe I shuld have been grateful at least one person in my life was uncomplicated enough to almost be considered a friend. Oliver was human, too.

I picked up my phone and scrolled through my contacts until I found the number Apollo had told me to reach him. After I called, it didn't take long before his loud bike roared down the road. When he stepped into my apartment, I wrapped my arms around his waist and buried my face against his chest. He closed his strong arms around me and held me.

"It'll be okay, angel."

I didn't need sex. I just longed for—companionship—to feel something other than the loneliness crippling my every thought. My lungs struggled for breath against ribs that felt like stone. With each passing day, I lost more of myself. My closest friend. Control. What was left? My biggest mistake was thinking nothing in my world would be affected. But now I felt like a shell, barren and losing grip on reality. I was desperate to forget about all the things that had been going wrong for a while.

I didn't think too hard about the fact I'd called one of the gods to spend time with me when I was in distress, rather than leaning on one of the humans. It was only proof I really was losing touch with my human side and seeing it manifest itself this way scared me. I was starting to feel distant from who I used to be, and I wasn't comfortable with it. Yet at the same time, being in Apollo's company felt right, and I didn't want to be anywhere else.

What if this happened every time I died? Until my last life where I died for real.

CHAPTER 12

Ares

I'd gone from sidekick to reject to messenger boy. Wasn't my time on Earth just exciting as hell? When I'd been sent to Earth by Zeus, it had been about fighting at Elyse's side.

Then she pushed me away because Zeus had never asked her if I was what she needed when she asked for help. This whole situation pissed me off but stewing about something wasn't my style. I was a man of action, always had been. Anything less was boring.

Now I was Heracles' errand boy because he was too busy with other shit? Fuck that. Why couldn't he talk to Elyse? This whole modern era was about technology and not speaking face-to-face. The age where any human being could contact any other with cell phones and the internet and everything else they'd invented to make the world smaller. Why couldn't Heracles use one of those instead of treating me like Hermes?

With fewer countries actually engaging in full on war, wasn't like I had anything better to do with my time. Besides, Elyse was someone I didn't mind spending time with and getting to know more about.

And Heracles was intimidating when he was in a shitty mood, which he had been when he asked me to look Elyse up. The guy had spent centuries training warriors. But he wasn't a bad guy and I had nothing against him, so I agreed to help him out. I heard how much he cared for Elyse in his voice.

When I arrived at the community center Heracles had sent me to—the same location I saw Hades exit when I followed him—Elyse was already warming up inside. I watched her for a moment. Her approach was systematic, running through one drill after the next, warming up certain muscle groups. It didn't take a trained eye to know she knew what she was doing, that working out was a very big part of her life.

Good. Dedication, and all that.

I pushed open the glass door, and she spun around. She frowned when she saw me.

"You're the last person I expected to walk through that door," she said.

I didn't ask her whom she'd expected. Heracles? Or maybe she would have liked to see Hades. I knew how he felt about her, but I was willing to bet that she felt something for him, too. Who could resist a god, right?

And I'd had my share of lovers, both mortal and deities, and something about Elyse had me curious to find out more about her.

Still, not something I was going to go into now. I was inquisitive, I'd admit, but it wasn't the place or time.

"Heracles is tied up," I said. "He's not going to make it for your workout."

"Tied up with what?" Elyse snapped, as if this wasn't the first time he'd let her down.

I shook my head. "Don't know, don't care. It's bad enough I'm doing his dirty work for him. I came to tell you my job is done."

"Gee, thanks," Elyse said. "You really put yourself out there, huh?"

"Are you being sarcastic with me?" This was unexpected. I hadn't seen this snappy side of her before, and something other than curiosity gripped me. She intrigued me as she didn't back down, not even to a god.

"I guess so," she said. She strolled to the other side of the room and picked up a Dragon's Punch, then she started swinging it around as if she knew what she was doing.

Weapons were my thing—war was so boring without them. And the Dragon's Punch happened to be one of my favorites. A beam of excitement flooded through me at seeing the way she handle it.

"I'll train with you," I offered, squaring my shoulders. I wanted to see what she could do with the thing. She was strong but seeing her wield the balls and chain was a total turn-on. Not that I would do anything about my reaction. She didn't exactly see me as that kind of person. But still, a man could fantasize.

"No, thank you," Elyse replied, focusing on her weapon.

"Are you scared?"

She laughed, her voice soft, stroking the length of my spine. "Of you?"

Oh, was that how it was going to be?

"Come on," I said, strutting toward her. She was still swinging the Dragon's Punch, and I dodged the weapon, nudging her hard enough on the shoulder that she lost her balance. Then I grinned at her.

Elyse glared at me, her mouth dropping at what I had done, and I gained myself a frown. Perfect.

"Cut the crap, Ares," she stated.

"Show me what you've got," I said, nudging her again.

She held her stance, her lips pulling tight. That was what I wanted—to pick a fight with her. I wasn't serious about starting anything with animosity, but I planned to draw her out. She was so tense, so uptight. Whatever was bugging her needed a release.

"You'll regret it," she warned.

I laughed, loud and for show. "There isn't very much I regret in this life."

"This life?" Elyse asked. "Like you had any other."

I tilted my head from side to side, cracking my neck, then bounced on the balls of my feet. "Come on. Let me see what you've got," I said.

She started swinging the Dragon's Punch, holding one ball in her left hand, the chain in her right. She struck out with the metal ball, and I dodged just before it would have hit like a steel fist. I retaliated, darting in between her and the metal ball, and she managed to parry my blow at the last moment.

"You could have broken my nose if I let you get me," Elyse spat, her voice almost shaken.

"Yeah. Good thing you blocked me."

I wasn't going to let up on her. She was extremely strong and deserved a worthy opponent. Besides, now we were fighting, I was in my element. I buzzed with adrenaline, contemplating releasing my war cry, but I didn't want to terrify the girl.

She swung the ball around and in an arc over her head before she slammed it down, aiming for me. The strike would have been deadly for any mortal, difficult to block but easy to avoid. I jumped out of the way and swung my leg around, kicking her in the ribs. She let out a grunt, but she didn't double up or go down. Impressive.

She did drop her weapon, though. Clumsy.

As soon as she was unarmed, I attacked. We started fighting. I kicked and punched and spun around, trying to get any open space to do damage. I didn't want to hurt her, but Elyse could handle herself. I heard she'd died once before, and since then, her power operated on a whole new level.

She managed to block most of my onslaughts and offered a few of her own. She only broke through once or twice.

When I knocked her off her feet, I ran for the Dragon's Punch, spun the weapon around, and threw the metal, spiked ball toward her, letting it land around her legs with a thump. She stumbled backward, landing on her back, then she slid across the floor toward me. I jumped forward and straddled her, pinning her down.

"This is where I could kill you," I declared, smirking at her.

"It's not that easy," Elyse retorted as she struggled against my hands holding hers down on either side of her. I was planning to let her go, but her body wriggled underneath mine, and awareness of her feminine form, the hard muscles under her smooth skin, stretched through me. Her wrists were tiny in my hands, her whole body as slender as she was strong. That lust from earlier returned with a vengeance. It slammed into me like a tornado, ripping my insides apart with only one focus—me getting closer to Elyse.

And this time, I didn't tell myself I wasn't going to act on it.

Because suddenly, I wanted to.

I leaned forward and kissed her. She froze under me when I did, as if she didn't know what to do.

But then she kissed me back, fast and furious. I

understood she was involved with Hades and Apollo. But I couldn't help myself. I craved this time with her. The energy wrapped around me, driving me to insanity if I didn't act on my desire. How could someone make me feel this way when I'd always been about the conquest, all about winning?

My cock was immediately hard in my pants, throbbing. And the scent of her arousal filled the room.

Elyse seized the moment I wasn't on my guard and pushed up, rolling me over so she had the upper hand. She was on me, now, pinning me down. She couldn't hold me for long, though.

I got out of her grip with ease, but the fight had become sexy. We played a game, wrestling on the ground, trying to avoid getting pinned, trying to get the other down. And I adored every touch, every grunt, every small twitch of her lips as if she might break into a smile.

And each time I had her, I kissed her. I ground my dick against her. I touched her, my hands sliding over her ass, her hips, her flat stomach, her breasts.

May the gods help me, I desired her. I wanted her so fucking badly.

She scrambled to her feet when she got away. I rushed at her and grabbed her, then I drove her backward until her back hit the mirrored against the wall. It cracked with the impact, but it didn't shatter.

I pinned her between my thighs, my back rounded so I could reach her face where she was more than a head shorter than me. And I kissed her, rolling my body against her, my erection against her lower stomach.

She moaned into my mouth when I slid my tongue over her lips, and I kissed her like I hadn't kissed a woman in over a hundred years.

Elyse tasted of war, of the sweat from our battle, the anger behind it. And she tasted like raw sex.

I slid my hand down her body, feeling her, touching her. I found her breast, squeezed it, pinched the nipple through her clothes. She whimpered beneath me, doing something to me, and I knew then and there I had to have her, or the need would drive me to madness.

She pushed her hands against my chest, but I wasn't ready to part. She took a couple of steps away from me, breathing hard.

"No, Ares," she said in a voice that commanded way more authority than the situation warranted. She was telling me to stop.

Fuck. This. Shit.

"We're not doing this," she said.

"Fine." My whole body humming with desire, yet my head screamed to end this. I was torn in two directions, and nothing made sense. Fuck, I needed fresh air. What was I doing? I stormed to the door.

"You're just leaving?" she asked.

"I know when I'm not wanted," I said, then left. Rejection was a slap in the face all by itself. I wasn't going to stand around waiting to be pitied, too. What the hell had I thought would happen? I wasn't the other gods she'd already given herself to. And Elyse was so much better than those lowly women I'd fucked before. Of course, it was my time to leave. I didn't need my life complicated by a woman right now.

I should have stuck to fighting. We would still have been going at it.

But I hadn't been able to help myself. Her body had been addictive—the art of war made it so much more tantalizing—and I had to admit I could see what Hades saw in her.

Almighty Zeus, but what a high it would be to plunge my dick inside her. Hades was one lucky bastard that he got to fuck her, and I didn't.

But, whatever. This wasn't my game, anyway. I would get over this little shitshow, probably find another woman or two to fuck to get it out of my system, and be done with the pent-up feelings. I wasn't here for Elyse. I was here because Zeus sent me. So, I'd do what was needed of me.

No need to complicate things or piss Zeus off even more. Those lightning bolts stung like a motherfucker, and I didn't want one shoved up my ass.

Really, no complications. Which was exactly what this whole story with Elyse and her boytoys was. A complication. It was simpler to stick to combat. The rules were simple there.

It was what I was best at, after all.

CHAPTER 13

Hades

I'd hoped after Elyse and I slept together, I'd have some kind of clarity about my obsession with her. Instead, everything was messed up, and I had no idea how I felt. Then again, I had gone there to talk to her about what was going on, not to fuck her. And now I had, I was back to square one. I liked her too much to turn my back and walk away.

But all this shit was too close to what I'd been through before to accept the tangled mess and move on. Besides, what if she had feelings for Poseidon? What if she actually liked him the way I liked her? I didn't know if I could deal with that—it was bad enough that Poseidon and Zeus always took what they wanted and didn't bother to find out if I wanted it first. It was so much worse this time. I knew what I desired, and they might still take it away from me. I was terrified of losing her, and it hurt like hell to know that was a massive possibility.

What pissed me off the most was I hadn't come to Earth to fall for someone. I'd arrived here to get away from Persephone, the woman who'd managed to rip out my heart without it actually being her fault. I'd come here to run away from everything that had gone wrong in my life. But instead of a break, I had only found a life more complicated.

And I definitely didn't want to get hurt again, to feel as if my heart was a crescendo of anger and anguish. Once was more than enough for a lifetime.

But it made me furious Poseidon was in the picture at all. I didn't want him here, getting involved in my business and definitely not to get involved with Elyse. Of course, if it was what she wanted, there was nothing I could do about it.

Which was why I had to talk to her. Again. Maybe this time I'd succeed. I needed to make sure that we were okay—if we weren't going to be together that way, maybe we could be friends.

Which was such a pussy line. I really had it for this girl if I was willing to be friends when I was head over heels for her. But that would be easier than fighting my brother for her all the time. Besides, I doubted Elyse actually wanted to be with me. I was good for a quick fuck, but I wasn't boyfriend material.

Ask Persephone.

My head swirled with so many regrets. I'd been tricked into so many of the situations. An insatiable fire burned through my body, leaving me empty. I left my home and headed out.

It took me a while to find Elyse. Not because I didn't know where she was, but because I had no clue what to say when I found her. So, I wandered the streets of the city, going everywhere but where she was.

When I finally decided to make my way to her apartment and knocked on her door, I felt like an idiot.

Someone opened the door next to hers, and a man popped his head out. He frowned at me. I half-expected him to demand to know who I was, but Elyse opened her door.

"Hades," she said, her voice shaky. "What are you doing here?"

She didn't sound very happy to see me. Great. It was already going wrong.

"I want to talk," I said.

Elyse nodded and widened the door, letting me into her apartment. I glanced at her neighbor before I stepped inside. She closed the door behind me.

"What?" Elyse asked, her hands folded over her chest. She eyed me with suspicion.

"I want to talk about the other day."

"You mean the sex?" she asked, her voice climbing.

I nodded. I wasn't sure what was going on. Elyse wasn't exactly angry, but she was very standoffish.

"I think we need to talk about it, don't you?" I asked.

"What is there to talk about?" she said flippantly as if it meant nothing more to her than a fun moment.

Something I'd normally do, except her tone was a blade to my gut. Plus, I was starting to get irritated.

"Are you being serious?" I said. "Are you just going to act like it was nothing? Or *was* it nothing?"

"Why are we back on this?" she asked, her posture stiff. "I already told you, I wasn't the one who was messing around. You left me in an office at the police station, for crying out loud!"

That was true, and it had been a dick move on my part. But I'd freaked out about what we'd done—about how strong my feelings had been. Getting together with her at all had been stupid. If I'd known it would cause so many problems, I'd never have done it.

"Look, if you're interested in my brother instead, tell me. I get it."

She sighed and walked away from me until she was on the other side of the coffee table, putting something between us. The symbolism wasn't lost on me.

"No, Hades, you don't get anything."

"Then tell me," I said.

Anything at this point would do as long as it wasn't this weird strained conversation. I wanted her to give me something I could go by.

"There's nothing to tell. What happened, happened." Yet her taut voice, void of emotions, told me it wasn't so simple. She was angry.

"And what now?" I asked. "Where do we go from here?"

She turned her head toward the window, not making eye contact with me. "There is no way to go. Let's face it. I'm here because of X and what he's doing. And you"—she looked at me—"are here because you want to rule the world. That puts me directly against you."

I shook my head. "You've got it all wrong."

"I doubt it. Don't think that for one moment I'm okay with you killing so many people. Even if you're hiding behind X to do it. And I haven't forgotten that you killed me, either. This just isn't the kind of game we can play—sex and death don't mix."

"So, what? Are you ending this?" I squared my shoulders, lifting my chin, refusing to let her see how much her words affected me.

"Ending what? There was never anything there. Remember?"

I grew more and more frustrated, the blaze within bubbling under my skin. Elyse was making this harder than it needed to be. I just wanted to know that we were okay, but apparently, we were everything but. And I supposed I couldn't blame her—if she thought I was behind the killings, of course she'd see me as the bad guy.

"X isn't mine to reel in, and no one seems to understand this," I growled.

She glared at me with narrowing eyes as if I lied.

And I was getting pretty damn sick of being made out to be the villain. I turned around and walked acros the room. Elyse tried to say something to me, but I yanked open the front door and stormed away before she could say anything else. I wasn't here to defend myself, to try to convince her I wasn't the bad guy. If she wanted to believe I was, so be it. I'd deal with being pushed aside.

I stalked down the road, fucking furious and itching for a fight. A good battle or a good fuck, that was what made my world go around. It took the edge off like nothing else could—not even wine or whatever else the humans poured into their bodies on a daily basis would suffice.

And seeing sex wasn't on the cards for the night—Elyse had been more than a bitch about it—it would have to be a fight.

Fuck.

Sex with her would have been pretty damn fantastic. Anything with her was incredible, though. Even if we'd just had a conversation, that would have been great. But whatever was eating her had stopped anything good from coming from the conversation I'd just had with her. So here I was alone, without a lover or even a friend.

I didn't even want to think what that all meant for her relationship with Poseidon. I was willing to bet everything I had Elyse wasn't like that with him. She'd never turn him down. Who would? Poseidon threw off such a huge fucking shadow, there was no way I could avoid walking in it. I should have known someone like Elyse was too good to be true.

What made it all worse was that it wasn't just Elyse who seemed to think I was the villain. Poseidon thought so too. They were all somehow convinced X was my problem.

The guy took a couple of souls here or there. It was hardly a train wreck.

I knew X. Talk about throwing off a shadow. That motherfucker was mine. Not exactly the kind of tail you'd want, but what was I going to do? When I'd inherited the Underworld, the worst of the worst came with the job, and I inherited Death.

So here I was with death on my heels—literally. And I somehow thought Elyse would look at me twice? I was delusional, that was all. I should have known nothing would come of this. I should have known it was only sex between us, and I should have taken her for the good fuck she was and left it at that.

Instead, I'd gotten all involved in the one way I'd told myself I'd never get involved with someone again. Well, that was going to end here and now.

I was so deep in thought I hadn't noticed where I was going. Without meaning to, I'd ended up downtown instead of the shitty neighborhood I'd chosen to stay in. And it was dark down here, even though it was daytime.

Which could only mean one thing.

"Any reason you're wandering around?" X grunted, seeing me before I saw him.

"Any reason you're actually making casual conversation with me?"

X was Death. He never made conversation because he usually killed whomever he came in contact with in the human world, and let's face it, the guy wasn't exactly Mr. Sunshine. This was strange.

"You're far from home, Hades," X said, a thousand whispers dancing on my skin.

Granted, he was right. I wasn't close to the Underworld, where I probably belonged. But he was far from home, too. And he was acting like I was out of line for being here. Before I could respond to him—the very idea of talking to the guy was weird—he disappeared.

He didn't just ghost into thin air like he usually did, though. His presence seemed to be a lot more stable on Earth now. That didn't look like it was a good thing. Was he changing?

As I watched, X moved from one shadow to the next, sliding over the ground like oil. When he'd moved a little farther, he pressed himself against the wall. If people thought the bogeyman was scary, well, this guy was a nightmare from hell.

An elderly couple walked past, holding hands, eating ice cream they'd just bought from a vendor.

X closed in on them, a dark cloud that wrapped around them. I stepped forward.

They were old, but it wasn't their time to go yet.

"X!" I shouted. But he didn't listen to me.

The Reaper inhaled, and a shiver slid up my spine. The old couple screamed. X swallowed their cries of despair, followed by what looked like mist coming out of their wide-open mouths. As I watched, he drew it all in and their bodies withered away, looking like they were decomposing, and soon there was nothing left of them but dust.

And the ice cream cones lying on the ground.

X had vanished.

I shuddered. This was all fucking wrong. Nothing was as it should have been. X wasn't behaving normally, even for going wild and eating souls. I'd never seen him do this before.

I closed my eyes and willed myself away. It took me a moment to steady my mind and body enough to make the trip. But finally, I ended up on the bank of the River Styx in the Underworld. The water formed a border between the world of the living and the dead. The sun was setting, as it always was here. Skeletal trees lined the banks on both sides while a pasty fog hovered over everything in sight. A wooden boat, with a lit lantern hanging from the carved skeletal head on the bow, bobbed in the water near the shore. Charon sat on a bench, looking out over the choppy river.

"Oh, it's you," he said, standing up. His black robes wafted gently in the breeze. "I was hoping for some business."

"It's been quiet?" I asked.

The hood moved, the only sign that he'd nodded. "No souls in here for a while. I've never been this bored."

Charon was the ferryman who took newly deceased souls over the River Styx to the Underworld, where I collected them. There were always at least a couple of souls per day coming in.

There had never been none, and that reality settled in my gut like a boulder.

This meant X wasn't doing his job and sending them to me. He was staying on Earth and he kept all those souls to himself. And I had no fucking idea why he was doing this or what he hoped to gain. But it worried me that he might continue to become so powerful even I couldn't stop him.

This was what they'd all been talking about. This was what they blamed me for. And seeing that X was usually part of who I was, this wasn't only worrying. It was a real shitty problem. How could I have not checked on this earlier?

CHAPTER 14

Elyse

The last few days I'd been completely distracted. I hadn't fought as much as I should have. In fact, I hadn't fought at all.

I'd been spending time with Apollo. I'd dreamed about Poseidon and his Hippocamps. I'd allowed myself to be a human for once and booked some downtime.

Even though I wasn't exactly a mortal anymore, I tried not to dwell on that too much. It only scared me to think I was starting to lose my connection with the person I used to be. The woman my father raised. I'd give anything to have my dad with me now, to hear his guidance on how to get myself out of the troubles I'd landed myself in.

I tried to remember if he'd ever felt this way, like he

was losing contact with who he'd been after he'd died. I saw him die once, and it was an event remained raw and terrifying in my memory. The event still ripped me up to see his lifeless eyes staring into the abyss. I'd screamed and run to his side after his fight where he'd been taken out by a griffin. Even though I knew he was going to come back, seeing him killed rocked me at the core, and it took me weeks to recover.

.

He'd come back to life later that day. I'd cried and he wrapped me in his arms and held me tight, warm and smelling like my dad always smelled. Musky and spicy.

He'd never changed. So why was I becoming someone else?

"We have to get back into training," Heracles said when I arrived at the training center for the first time in a few days. I'd paused my workout, too. I was burning out. The work I was doing consumed me until there was nothing else left.

That, and the fact that my mind had been all over the place after what happened with Ares, and then with Hades almost immediately after. I had no idea where I stood anymore.

"I've been running," I told him. I'd had to keep up my fitness. I couldn't afford to give it all up.

"It's not enough." Heracles's face grew serious. He

stood there, tanned and perfect and looking like something was seriously wrong. The opposite of the night I'd gone to this place in fear after X threatened me.

"Have you been watching the news?" he insisted.

I shook my head. I'd kept the television off because I knew if I saw something, I'd be sucked in.

"X is stronger than he was. Worse. If you want any chance to actually take him down, you need to up your game."

I swore under my breath. "I can never catch a break from danger, can I?"

"Not while X is here, no." Heracles came toward me and handed me the Dragon's Punch I'd been training with. It had become my favorite weapon.

"This is going too far," I said when we started our warmup. "No one seems to care about it other than me."

"No one else can stop him," Heracles said.

I shook my head. "I don't believe that. Why would Zeus not be able to do something about it?"

"Do you know what my uncle did to me when I was a kid?" Heracles asked. The question was out of the blue, but I nodded.

"He made you human or something," I responded.

"Yeah, to kill me. So I wouldn't stop him from releasing the Titans to destroy the world. My own uncle wanted to kill me. And the only thing Zeus was able to do about it—about stopping his own brother—

was to teach me who I really was so I could stop him. Because such a task was my destiny, not his."

I breathed hard, doing all the warmup exercises while Heracles stood to the side. He didn't have to train, but even if he did, he wouldn't break a sweat.

"So, he can't do anything about X because..." I began for him.

"Because it's not his destiny. It's yours."

I shook my head. "The gods are the most powerful beings, but they're held back by destiny? It seems pathetic if you ask me."

Heracles shrugged. "It's the foundation of our existence. We can't help it. Even the humans who believe they can create their own fate, and try to, end up on the path they were destined for. Even if they think it's their own doing."

It sounded like no one had any kind of say then. Which I didn't like. Heracles spoke about humans creating their own destiny as an adorable attempt in futility.

"I'll do something about X," I said.

"Like what?" he asked.

"I'll figure it out."

I drank water after warming up and we got down to training. Heracles didn't let up, and I was glad. I needed him to give it to me hard. And the intensity helped me forget my dreaded thoughts of the men in my life.

After training, I got in my car and drove to the park, sweaty and my muscles aching. I took a few photos of the leaves changing color, of kids playing. I drove into town and took a photo or two of graffiti on the walls, of rubbish blowing in the street. Anything that would give me a break when I actually had to focus on work for a change. To make myself feel as normal as possible.

Then I went in search of Ares. He was full of shit and we'd parted on a weird footing—he'd been pissed I'd said *no* to sleeping with him. But I wouldn't have been able to do a fourth gods in as many weeks. Or however long it had been. I'd lost track of time.

When I stumbled upon him, he was on a park bench, looking ready for trouble. He had short-cropped hair and sore baggy camouflage pants with a tight T-shirt. And was he smoking?

"That's not something gods usually do," I said, referring to the cigarette.

He shrugged and threw the butt on the ground, stubbing it out with his toe.

"What do you want?" he asked, not looking my way.

"A fight."

He glanced up at me with suspicious eyes.

"Not with you. With X. I need you to stick with me so we can take this guy down and out for good. I'm getting sick of him tearing up my town."

I expected Ares to say *no*. I'd blown him off and bruised his ego, I knew that. But he jumped up and rubbed his hands together. "Finally. I'm so fucking bored." He smirked, and the spark in his eyes returned.

I chuckled. "Okay."

X wasn't hard to track down. We traveled through the city until I picked up his energy vibrations. Downtown, his essence was so strong, it was like walking into the night when we found him. I didn't want to think about how he'd gotten this strong. The more souls he devoured, the heavier the darkness hung around him.

So many innocents. I'd been an idiot to think I could take a break from all of this, stick my head in the sand as if that would make it all go away.

"X!" I shouted when we spotted him in the midst of the darkness, a storm that swirled with terror. His eyes burned with blue flames instead of the churning orange they'd been before.

When he stared at me, I stared at his chest. There was no way I'd make eye contact with him ever again. I had the sickening feeling that if I did, my mind would be his. Not my soul, because that would never belong to him with Zeus' power in my veins. But my mind was far too much for him to own.

"You're done here," I said. It was hard to act tough while staring at his chest. A lot of intimidation came with eye contact. But I wasn't going to test the theory about X that was rolling around in my mind.

"I thought I told you to stay out of my way," he hissed. "And you brought backup. Or something. He's not the best you could find, is he?"

"Fuck," Ares said under his breath, and I glared at X. Bastard was playing with us.

"Let's get this over with," I snarled to Ares. "I need you at my back."

"Got it," Ares declared.

I had my Dragon's Punch with me and I swung it around. It was a weapon that wasn't easy to see coming. I still had my blades with me, but this was going to make a difference.

"Do you think your toys are going to help?" X asked and chortled like a hyena.

I'd never heard him laugh before, and I hoped I'd never hear it again. The sound was creepy and warm, but when it touched my skin it felt like a wire brush. It hurt, too. Like I'd been burned.

I flicked the Dragon's Punch at him, but he stepped to the side. I yanked the ball back and caught it.

X laughed again. Fuck, I really wanted him to stop that.

"What is your sidekick doing?" he asked.

I looked over my shoulder at Ares. He was surrounded by light and it was spectacular to see, although it wasn't what we had planned. Instead of staying behind me as I'd asked, he shot past me with a loud cry and attacked X. Guess he took his instruction from Zeus about having my back as meaning he did the fighting.

The light drove away the darkness in a sense. But not enough. X rose, and the darkness rose with him like a wave, growing until it was so thick, I couldn't see my own hand before my face.

"This isn't going to work." Ares grunted. When I glanced around, he seemed different than usual. Taller, more muscular. Scarier.

And were those horns on his head? Ares had transformed into some kind of devil, with scaly skin and thick armor, eyes that glowed jade green. That was right, Ares could shapeshift. I'd learned this, but I'd never seen a god do it in reality. It had all been theory until about five seconds ago.

Watching him battle was spectacular. He could fly, too. And he lifted himself off the ground now, shooting into the air, his body a bullet, his momentum making him deadly.

He attacked X with a vengeance I hadn't seen before.

And it would have been perfect if this was a one-man show and we hadn't had a plan. But Ares should have had my back, like I'd asked. I'd intended to engage X and Ares could pick up the slack. But I'd take what I had, so we could make this work. I rushed forward when X slammed Ares into the ground, creating a crater in the Earth. I cringed. When he pulled back and came after me, Ares didn't rise again. I knew that the god couldn't be dead—if they could take each other out, there would be very few gods left. But he was out of action for the moment.

And I was alone. Which was exactly what I hadn't wanted to be. Darkness closed in around me, and a small light beamed from my chest, coming from Apollo's necklace.

X hissed, but it didn't stop him. The fog closed in around my throat, and my breaths refused to come.

"I told you I'm going to end you for getting in my way," X snarled. His voice was like the wind, tugging at my hair, pushing into my mouth when I tried to gasp for air. The promise terrified me, and I clawed at my neck, but my fingers fell through the mist. Yet a tightness squeezed. Panic gripped me as reality tapped into my brain. I could die here. Helpless.

I was under no illusion that X couldn't rip me apart if. And yeah, so I would respawn. That was great. But who said he wouldn't do it again? And again and again and again. Until it was all over.

"Thanatos!" someone bellowed, and we both turned our heads.

Poseidon stood in all his glory, wind tugging at his hair and clothes, the crack of thunder rumbling behind him. It felt as if the air inhaled, and the constriction on my neck eased. I breathed in deeply, trapping the energy in my lungs, recoiling.

"I haven't heard that name in centuries," X said.

His voice grated on my nerves like television static.

"I had to get your attention somehow, you bastard," Poseidon sneered.

That's right, Death had a Greek name. The god of Death was called Thanatos, but we all called him 'X' because it was easier to remember.

Poseidon darted toward us. His trident glinted in his hand, his face was riddled with anger and only when X withdrew and the darkness let me go did I realize Death had held me in his clutches, darkness seeping into my very pores. Panic sliced through me.

I fell to the ground. I didn't see how Poseidon did it, but there was a mighty crack that lit up the sky and a scream that curdled my blood before everything died down.

"Elyse," Poseidon called, and I looked around to find him.

The skies weren't so dark anymore. X had fled and the air exhaled.

CHAPTER 15

Poseidon

We lost that fight. I'd come in the nick of time—X had been about to kill Elyse. An ache had settled under my heart when I saw how close he was to killing her. I couldn't lose her, and with that thought, a primal fear shuddered through me. What if he'd succeeded? I ran him off, but there was no way we'd won anything in this war. All I accomplished was buying us time, and sparing one of Elyse's lives.

Hers were so extremely precious, and my arms trembled by my sides with the urgency to take her into my embrace and never let her go. She only had a few lives. Thank Zeus she didn't only have one like any other mortal or I would have lost her before finding her. She could only die two more times, and I'd lose her forever. That thought sat heavily on my chest, churning through me in tense cramps. Not much scared me, but now, fear shackled me, hammering on my head. If I hadn't found her in time, she'd be gone.

Coupled with my dread, a fire surged within me that she risked her life so easily.

"What do you think you're doing?" I demanded, fury burning me up on the inside. My power crackled in the air around me, lifting the hairs on my arms.

Elyse looked surprised I was upset, her eyes widening.

"What I was sent here to do," she said simply, as if never once doubting her decision to place herself in danger.

"You could have died! What do you think this is? A game?" My voice climbed, and I gritted my teeth, reminding myself to hold back the fury.

"Excuse me?" she asked incredulously. Her rage was rising; I could feel it mix with mine until the air around us was tainted with colors of anger and rage. "I'm doing what I was born to do. Zeus didn't make me this strong to just sit around."

"You should have waited for backup," I snapped.

"I had backup!" She pointed at Ares, staring at us, arms folded over his chest. "But he attacked X on his own and got slammed to the ground."

I followed her gaze to the hole in the ground where X had shown Ares that he wasn't nearly as good as he thought he was.

"Don't even get me started on him." I huffed and

stared at my trident. I was righteously pissed off he'd attacked X alone. Idiot. Moron.

"Zeus gave you power, but you're not a god, Elyse. You can still die." I wanted to cry as the realization filled me that I could have lost her. And that paralyzing hurt spread within me like ice.

"And bounce back again." She smirked.

"Only a couple times before it's over!" Heat scorched my neck and over my ears, and I trembled with fury. The anger was rooted in fear—what if I lost her?—but I wasn't going to admit to that.

"So, you want me to sit back and let all this shit happen? When I can do something about it? Because you're worried the final death will come too soon?" She studied me with narrowing eyes as if trying to read my thoughts, which was impossible.

Plus, my argument sounded pathetic when she said it like that, but what was I supposed to do? Congratulate her on not dying? Yet the niggling reminder sat on my mind that us gods had left X get away with this for too long, and instead of bickering, we had to come together and address the problem.

"I'm not saying you can't fight," I said. "I just want you to wait for backup. X is growing stronger, which means we need to work as a team."

"I already told you I had backup."

Ares sauntered toward us like he hadn't just had his ass handed to him by Death himself. Earlier, he'd been in one of his inhuman forms when he was in the crater, but now he looked normal again, with his short-cropped hair and his eyes laughing as if this were one big fat joke.

"Well, that was a colossal failure," Ares said mockingly, like it was no big fucking deal.

"You think?" I snarled. "Do you want to be a part of this team or are you set on doing whatever the hell you want?"

"Hey," Ares said, holding up his hands. "Why are you getting mad at me?"

"Because you need a leash," I snapped.

"He was here to fight with me, no questions asked," Elyse said.

"Don't defend him!" I glared at both of them.

I sounded like the father who lectured everyone, but I was furious. Their mistake chewed me up, and I couldn't help myself. I'd picked up the pieces for years. *Old habits die hard.*

"Look, man. I was just doing what Zeus sent me here to do," Ares declared, gripping his hips, staring at me as if he'd been asked to simply babysit Elyse.

Yeah, it was all about duty, huh?

"No, you were doing whatever you wanted." I snarled. "You just battle, Ares. You never fight for anything. Get a cause for a change."

"What do you think this was?" Ares's voice climbed, his chest puffing out. His green eyes had darkened. He was getting pissed too. Great, we had enough of us angry that we could hold a party.

"I think you're enjoying yourself because you got to punch something for a change. But you're not reliable. You never stand up for anything other than your own whims. You're a coward, Ares."

His face darkened and his eyes blazed such a bright green, it cast a shadow on Elyse's face.

"Fuck you, Poseidon," he said, and he ghosted away.

Of course he did.

Elyse and I were left alone.

"Well done," she said, arching a brow, judging me with that stare. "You did a great job of running him off."

I sighed. The anger drained out of my system, and I felt like an ass. "I shouldn't have said that."

Elyse shook her head. "I was fine on my own."

"You weren't," I replied. "You're bleeding."

Elyse studied the gash on her side that spilled blood on her clothes, and her arm was equally cut up. "Hell! Why do I only feel this pain now?" she asked, blanching.

"Adrenaline and power do well to hide it," I said. "Come on. Let's get you home."

Elyse nodded. I put my arm around her and took her back to her apartment in a flash. She pulled off her shirt and sat in her bra in the bathroom while I dressed her wound. Her cheeks were white, and she seemed miles away. Thank Zeus it was only a flesh wound and nothing more serious.

I cleaned her arm, kneeling before her where she

sat on the edge of the bath. Something about her innocence drove me to keep her safe, to guard her, to try to talk sense into her.

"Thank you," she said when I finished. "I usually just clean my wounds myself. It's kind of nice to have someone else care for me."

I nodded and looked up at her, understanding how lonely it must get for her. She was the only one left of her family, unable to tell anyone about her line of work. And I pitied her. Though I'd never admit it out loud. Right then, I toyed with the idea of cradling her in my arms, insisting I'd fight all her battles for her. Yet I somehow doubted she'd appreciate such an offer. She was powerful, independent, and feisty. Only a few of the things I adored about her.

"I've bandaged myself many times after battle. It was my alone time to consider what I'd done, what my next move was," she said.

Her dark eyes narrowed, and I put my hands on her legs. "But that's nothing compared to having someone close to help," I told her. "And I can't have you bleed to death."

Silence fell between us, and I ran the backs of my fingers across her cheek. "What are you thinking?"

"You'll call me silly, but I keep remembering the chariot ride with the Hippocamps." She shrugged. "It just made me forget everything, and I laughed so much. Something about having you there made me feel secure. That's weird, right? I've always looked after myself since Dad passed."

I cupped the side of her face. "Everyone needs joy in their life, and if that means taking you on rides in my chariot, I'll take you daily across the seas and show you the most wondrous of creatures and the most glorious sunrises across the watery horizon. Maybe even get you in the water next time." I winked.

She laughed, the sound soft and sexy. "You've got yourself a deal."

The atmosphere shifted between us, and I realized she was half-naked, and we were alone together. Intimate. I rose to my knees and Elyse opened her legs wider so I could move between them, calling me to her. I put my hand on her chin and kissed her. Her mouth was soft. I started gentle, just a brush of our lips, but she sighed and opened her mouth, and I slid my tongue into her. She tasted like water, something sensual.

My arms slid around her body and I drew her closer to me, careful not to hurt her. Her legs closed around my waist and her crotch pressed up against mine. My erection grew thick in my pants, responding to the feel of her skin under my hands, she nestled against me.

I broke our kiss and moved down her body, moving her hair out of the way as I made my way down her neck and onto her chest. The bra she wore was in my way and I fiddled with the clasp. Damn human invention. Bras were the curse of the past couple centuries.

When I managed to unhook it, I peeled the fabric from her shoulders and dropped it on the floor.

Her breasts were pure perfection. I cupped them, licking the soft skin on the swell before I moved my hand and sucked one nipple into my mouth.

Elyse moaned and buried her hands in my hair. I loved the way her fingers kneaded on my scalp.

I moved from one nipple to the other, the nubs hard in my mouth, her gasps and moans filling the bathroom.

When I couldn't hold it in anymore, I let go of her and took her hand. I stood and led her out of the bathroom to her bedroom. I kissed her again, our bodies molded together. I gyrated my hips, pressing my cock against her. My hands slid down her back, cupping her ass.

Elyse traced her fingers down my body and undid the buttons on the shirt I wore.

"Always so formal," she murmured.

I shrugged. When she opened the shirt, she pressed her hands against my skin, her fingers in my chest hair. I took a deep breath and sighed.

She slid the shirt off my shoulders, and when she hugged me, her naked breasts pressed against my bare chest.

I fumbled with her pants, undoing the zipper, and she sat down, letting me pull them off her legs one by one. I kissed her smooth skin when they were bare, moving my way up toward the apex of her thighs.

Elyse lay back and her thighs fell open for me. When I met her gaze, her eyes were almost all pupil. I dove between her legs and licked a line from her entrance to her clit. She cried out. I closed my mouth over her clit and sucked.

She writhed beneath me on the bed, and I loved it. Her body was everything a goddess's body should be. My dick stood so rock hard, it hurt. I wanted to bury it inside her.

But not yet.

My hands wandered over her legs, her ass, over her stomach, and to her breasts as I licked and flicked her. I pinched her nipples and tugged at them while I worked her over, and she moaned, her body shuddering. Her skin was warm and smooth, and I lapped at her until she orgasmed against me. She thrashed, and I loved seeing her lose control under my influence.

The pleasure that washed over her was intense, and she cried out, tilting her body to the side, closing her legs around my head. They held me there, and I didn't let up. I licked her, sucking, kissing her pussy lips until she breathed hard, collapsing her legs to the sides.

"You're so beautiful," I said.

I stood, letting her recover on the bed. I undid my pants and dropped them to the floor, kicking off my boots.

Elyse sat up while I was undressing. She studied my dick, standing at attention, waiting to be relieved. Reaching out a hand, she brushed over my hardness, and my cock twitched and bumped against her touch. She ran her fingers around the head, her other hand tickling my thighs. I groaned and caressed her face, running my fingers through her long hair. It had been in a braid while she'd fought, but it was loose now, a dark waterfall down her back.

When she leaned forward, she pressed her mouth against my head and I growled under my breath. My fist closed in her hair, tangling my fingers in as she moved deeper onto my dick, drawing it into her mouth.

Her mouth was hot on my shaft, soft against the head as she rolled her tongue around me. I gasped with arousal.

"I won't last if you do that," I moaned.

"Try," she said with a cheeky voice, pulling back to talk before she sank back onto me. Pulling me deeper into her mouth, her hands on my balls and on my stomach, she massaged me. I tipped my head back.

"Fuck," I bit out when she started bobbing her head back and forth, pumping my dick in and out of her mouth, making me want to lose my load here and now. But this was far from over, and I wasn't going to let this end here.

My hands were still in her hair, and I had to hold back from keeping her in place and pushing down her throat, fucking her face. Elyse deserved more than that. And I'd finish in her mouth for sure if I did that.

I pulled back.

"You're too much," I said with a growl, drawing her up by her elbows to kiss her. My tongue was in her mouth, but it wasn't enough. Not nearly. I reached between her legs and found her entrance, pushing my fingers into her.

"You're so wet," I said.

Elyse moaned against my lips.

I spun her around, pressing my dick against her perfect ass. I slid my hands over her throat. Her neck was tiny, the skin smooth, and I traced her collar bones with my fingers. She turned her head and kissed me again. I gave her what she wanted, but just for a moment before I put one hand on her waist and the other on her back. I pushed her over, holding her hips so she bent over the bed for me. Her ass was round, her back long and smooth, and her hair hung over her shoulders to the mattress.

I found her entrance with my fingers again and used my other hand to guid my cock to her. When I plunged into her, Elyse cried out. I pulled her up again, using her arms, and when she was against me, she shuddered. My dick was buried inside of her and we fit together like we'd been made for each other. I wrapped one arm around her body, kept the other on her hips, and started moving inside her.

Elyse's body was the sexiest thing I'd seen in a long time, and she felt like velvet around my dick when I moved. I reached down her body, sliding away from her breasts and pressing a finger against her clit while I fucked her. It caused her hips to buck and pushed me deeper into her. She let out a breathy moan, and I fucked her harder. her hips bucked against me, my finger running in circles around her clit.

Her body spasmed and clamped down on my cock. I groaned. This was too good and I didn't want to finish.

She collapsed forward on the bed, and I pulled out. She lay down on the mattress and rolled onto her back when I nudged her. Her smile was the sexiest grin I'd seen. "I love the way you feel inside me."

"That's only the beginning, beautiful." I crawled over her, her legs opened for me again, and I thrust into her. This time, our bodies were mashed together, our faces only an inch apart. Her dark eyes were on mine, filled with lust and passion and everything I'd felt while I was with her.

This wasn't fucking. Until now, it had been. But this was more sensual. Something in me beamed with excitement and a joy I hadn't felt in too long. And I missed feeling so alive.

I started moving inside of her, stroking in and out. My eyes were locked on hers. I brushed my fingertips against her cheek and her mouth curled into a smile around her gasps. I pressed my lips against hers.

When I couldn't keep it slow anymore, I started moving faster again. I drove into her a little less gently. She tipped her hips up to meet mine. I pinned her to the bed, crushing her tiny frame with my large body.

But Elyse was strong, and when I looked at her, her eyes were filled with greed and lust, and I wanted to give it all to her. I was no longer merely buried inside of her; somehow, I felt like I'd become part of her.

I drew out and hammered into her again, hard, pushing in deeper. She gasped as if I was expelling all the air out of her. "Don't stop," she pleaded.

Her eyes were filled with dirty things, and I did it again, giving her more, taking what I craved. I pumped into her, grinding, thrusting, my muscles tight and flexing over her. We breathed hard in unison, grunting and moaning and gasping as I bucked my hips, ramming into her tight pussy.

When I was close, I pressed my lips against her mouth and plunged into her as far as I could. My body spasmed, my cock kicked out, and I started pumping into her, releasing everything that had built up since we'd kissed the first time.

She moaned out loud just after I came and her body convulsed around mine, my orgasm pushing into hers. She squirmed against me. Her eyes were still on mine, filled with great intensity, dark and serious.

Eventually, the orgasms died down and we lay, breathing hard, connected to each other, perfectly still. I kissed her again.

When I withdrew, I lay down beside her and rolled her against me, holding her tightly, never wanting to release her. And I could have lost her to X, but I refused to think of that now.

"I shouldn't feel this strongly about you." Having her in my embrace felt so right.

"But you do," Elyse answered as if she had indeed read my mind.

I nodded.

"Stay with me tonight?" Elyse asked. "I don't want to be alone. And you make me feel safe and adored."

I nodded again. I didn't intend to leave her anyway.

The gods weren't supposed to fall for mortals. But Elyse wasn't just a human. And she wasn't a goddess. But I could work around that.

For her, I would.

"Actually," I said. "I wanted to take you somewhere special, if you're up to it?"

She twisted around, glancing at me with curiosity behind her eyes. "I'd love that."

CHAPTER 16

Elyse

"I want to show you something."

Poseidon offered me his hand, palm upward, fingers outstretched toward me. He stood naked at the end of my bed, staring down at me. His eyes twinkled, and the corners of his mouth twitched.

What was he so excited about? We just had the most amazing sex, and now that glint in his gaze returned.

I reached out to accept him, and the moment our fingers touched, a spark sizzled between us. My world went black, then there was a bright light blinded me, and I shaded my eyes. I blinked until my vision settled. The sun sat low in the bright blue sky. Cool water lapped at my feet. And my toes wriggled in the sand. In front of me lay an enormous ocean, turquoise and so pure that it called to me to jump in. I longed to feel its embrace, dunk myself into its soft waves. The water glinted beneath the sunlight as if it were an opened treasure box, filled with jewels as far as the eye could see.

I glanced over to Poseidon who stood tall alongside me, wearing only knee-length shorts as if he might be a surfer. They seemed strange on him, yet when I glanced down at myself, I wore the tiniest green bikini. In truth, I owned only one swimsuit and it was a full piece, but this was gorgeous. I touched the sparkling fabric that seemed to be made of scales. My hair sat in a ponytail, out of my face, and fluttered in the breeze at my back.

"You like it?" Poseidon asked.

"Well, it's not leaving much to the imagination." I tugged on the material, revealing a lot of side boob.

I looked up at him, but he was glancing out at the great expanse of water. He was referring to the scenery, not the outfit that he'd dressed me in, and probably for the best he wasn't thinking I'd complained about the bikini.

Behind us, white sand stretched outward toward a green lawn and palm trees grew everywhere. Farther still lay homes and a road with cars driving past.

The familiarity of the area hit me fast. "I know this place. We're in Honolulu."

"Yes," Poseidon confirmed. "Your father brought you here for a holiday."

"How did you know I'd been here before, with Dad?" I asked.

Two months after my mother passed, Dad took us on a trip, insisting we needed to remember to continue with our life and not wallow in grief. I had an incredible time. We went snorkeling with turtles, toured the pineapple plantation, and even attended a couple of ghost tours. I swam every single day, convinced I'd morph into a mermaid.

"Some of the most beautiful beaches in the world are in Hawaii," Poseidon said. "But I know this place is special to you for a different reason, and I want to show you something." He took my hand in his, our fingers threaded together, and drew me into the sea. My heart beat so fast. How did he know this place meant to so much to me?

Cool waters swallowed my legs the deeper we traveled, and soft undulating waves rolled against us. "Are we swimming out into the ocean?" I asked.

Poseidon drew me toward him, smiling so wickedly it heated my insides. His hands clasped my hips and he lifted me to reach his face with ease. I wrapped my legs around his waist, my arms hanging around his neck.

"So, this thing you're showing me?" I teased. "Is it in your pants?" I laughed, unable to help myself at how dorky I sounded, but this beach brought me so much joy.

Being silly came with the territory as did just

having fun for the sake of enjoying myself far away from our troubles.

The smirk on Poseidon promised so many dirty answers, but instead he kissed me. He tasted sweet and salty. His mouth pressed against mine, one hand on my back, the other sliding to my ass. If anyone could make me forget my troubles, it would be a god.

The waves reached our shoulders yet Poseidon walked us deeper still. I was captivated, lost in his passion, focused on his hardness settled between my legs. Only two layers of fabric kept us completely apart, and despite the cold water, my skin burned hot.

He broke our kiss, when we were fully underwater, submerged in the crystal blue sea. I froze at first, my lungs locked up with the instinct to hold my breaths, my muscles tensing with the need to swim to the surface.

"Just take a normal breath," Poseidon insisted, holding me tight against him. An air bubble sat around his head as if he wore an oxygen helmet. And I raised to hand to my face, noticing inches from touching my nose, my fingers dripped with water. I wore the same bubble.

I heaved a deep inhale, drawing air into my lungs, not water. An excited tingle started at the base of my stomach that somehow I was breathing under water. My body was submerged, but my head remained dry. Poseidon grinned my way.

"Best way to enjoy the sea." His voice echoed as if we stood inside a tunnel.

A huge turtle swam past us, and I stared in awe. Coral and tiny fish of every color covered the seabed, and I pushed away from Poseidon, floating, turning myself around on the spot, admiring the beauty. A whole different world existed under the waves. I'd never once given it a second thought, but now I wanted nothing more than explore the ocean.

Poseidon swam into my view, waving for me to follow. We weren't deep under the sea, so the sunlight still filtered down, creating a magical glow.

Swimming after him, I glided through the waters, and each wave overhead tugged me from side to side. Poseidon landed near an oversized boulder, and he dropped to his knees, glancing my way. His hair flowed back and forth from the current, and I kicked my legs to reach him, excitement fluttering in my gut. He took my hand and drew me to his side with ease while I struggled to hold myself in one place. With his arm locked around my waist and our sides pressed together, I kneeled beside him in front of the rock. The surface was covered in mollusks and barnacles. Was he hoping to find an oyster with a pearl? I honestly had no clue what he intended to show me, but anticipation wove through me.

"Honolulu is one of my favorite spots on Earth," he said, "though I prefer to spend my time underwater and away from all the drama in Mount Olympus. One time, many years ago, when I came here and dove into these waters, something called to me like a beacon, and tiny vibrations found me. I tracked the source to this rock with no idea what it meant at the time, but when you told me your dad brought you to Honolulu, and I remembered the photo of you and your mom at your place, everything made sense." He looked at me with the biggest smile. "Our fates are tangled."

"How so?" My stomach fluttered at the implication.

He leaned forward and ran his thumb over something near a crusted shell stuck to the stone. I shifted closer, spotting something silvery. Reaching over, I fingered the object and the tiny ridges across the surface. "What is it?"

Poseidon pulled me closer to him for a better look.

I stared down and uncovered an oval locket with a sea shell engraved on the front. My breath caught in my throat.

"This is my mom's. She always loved the sea. But I lost the necklace when I was here with Dad!" My mind whirled with how I'd dropped it when I swam in the sea and never found the locket again, and the weeks I cried after losing the piece. How in the world Poseidon found the object? Fiddling with it, but I couldn't open the locket as half remained embedded in a mollusk.

"I was meant to find this for you. When I saw your mom wearing this locket in the photo in your apartment, I knew I had to show you what I found." He kissed my brow while my throat thickened.

I remembered my mother and her laugh, her strong hugs, how Dad had given me the locket on the day of her funeral and how I'd lost it, never forgiving myself.

"I can pry it free for you." When he moved to do so, I caught his hand and drew it to my chest.

"No, don't. Honolulu has always held a special place in my heart, and..." I paused for a moment, trying to find my words, to blink away the tears. "With Mom's locket now part of the ocean, it kind of feels like it belongs here. She loved the beach so much. This location not only holds wonderful memories about my dad for me, but whenever I visit now, it will now also represent my mother. And I love that I have a place for them both that brings back happy memories. Not just tears."

Poseidon pivoted me to face him, chest to chest, and I drowned in his eyes. They held so much passion behind them as if only I existed in this world. "That's beautiful, and I promise to bring you here as often as you wish."

Resting my cheek against his strong chest, I let myself soften into his embrace. There was a calmness about the sea, and now I understood why Poseidon wanted to spend his time here. Who didn't want such a sanctuary?

CHAPTER 17

Elyse

When I opened my eyes, I was alone. The bed next to me was empty and cold. Poseidon was gone.

I rolled onto my back and sighed. Why did this happen so often? The gods seemed to love disappearing after sex, even when I asked them to stay. Though I couldn't believe he'd found Mom's locket and surprised me with it. That touched my heart, and his actions showed a god full of compassion and love. I adored him for that.

Poseidon had been very serious about how he felt about me yesterday. He approached everything with rational thinking, never just jumping in. Maybe he'd be a good influence on me. And I couldn't ignore that he had a protective vibe that did something sexy for me.

Or rather, I knew how I felt about him and that scared me.

I was already involved with Apollo. And what about Hades, and the way we ended up colliding so often in ways I couldn't resist? He was Poseidon's brother. That was asking for a disaster.

The kiss with Ares wasn't even something I allowed myself to think about. It had been so intense, everything I would have let myself indulge in if it had just been the two of us. But since I'd met the gods, there had always been one, two, three too many players in this game.

And I had no idea what to make of it. Catina had voiced her opinion on my many, many attractions, had said it was wrong, but I didn't see why I couldn't care for more than one man at the same time. Except such a relationship required all of their consent. I huffed and drew the sheet to my chin, staring up at my white ceiling, wishing I'd woken up with Poseidon next to me. He'd distract me from thoughts and questions I had no answers to.

At least I felt as more stable with Apollo and what we meant to each other. That was one less problem I had to deal with and figure out. If I ignored the whole Zeus-potentially-ripping-him-away-from-me thing. Yep, nothing in my life was ever simple.

Not that I could see someone like Poseidon as a problem. He was everything that was good and gentlemanly in this world. But being with him just seemed to come with so many complications. It was all me, though. Not him. He was as straightforward as they got.

I pushed up in bed, shoved the bedsheet aside, and groaned. I ached all over, as if I'd been hit by a freight train. When I looked down my naked body, I was an artwork of bruises. Especially around the wound on my side. Poseidon had patched me up with gauze and bandages—it paid to have a medical kit when I fought as often as I did—but the purple marks flowered all around the dressing, a reminder that something awful was beneath it.

X had done this when he'd put his hands on me. Even though his touch hadn't hurt at the time, I understood he'd caused the bruises. No one got away from Death without a scratch.

I'd been too high on adrenaline during the fight, ready to lay myself down for the good of mankind. But my wounds hurt like a bitch now.

When I stood, my head swam, and nausea twisted at the pit of my stomach. I pressed my fingers against my lips and prayed I wouldn't retch. Just the thought of heaving when my muscles hurt so much was already painful.

I dragged myself to the bathroom to relieve myself, my thighs sensitive after my night with Poseidon—raw in the best way.

When I stared in the mirror, I had a bruise on my

jaw and a nice black eye. Perfect. I hadn't even seen that until now.

Poseidon hadn't seemed to care about me looking like I'd been beaten.

He'd brought me back to my place to take care of me. Neither of us had ulterior motives. But we hadn't been able to stay away from each other. It hadn't been the desperate lust we'd had for each other before—this had been soft and gentle. But it had been extremely strong. There was no way I could deny my feelings for him. Everything about Poseidon was attractive, from the way he looked to the way he acted toward me and the way he made me feel. He brought out an intensity that made me desire him in every sense of the word. Hell, he'd taken me for a ride on his chariot… how could I ever forget such an experience, his affection, the way he'd looked into my eyes while we'd had sex? I'd been lost in his world, and staying there sounded incredible.

But I also couldn't ignore my attraction to Hades, even though he always seemed to do something to piss me off. The guy was a divine pain in my ass. But I couldn't keep from letting him fuck me whenever we fought each other. He was a weakness my willpower was fragile against. Saying *no* to him seemed an impossibility.

How would Poseidon feel about me being intimate with Hades? Did he know about me and Hades? And about Apollo? And my kiss with Ares? Though I wasn't going to lose Apollo, so Poseidon would have to fit in.

God, was I seriously thinking about dating multiple guys at the same time? I covered my face and shuddered. If I could, I would. I was already sleeping with three of them. It'd been a close call or it would have been a fourth. I'd craved Ares so desperately, and if I'd kissed him a second longer back in the training hall, I'd have been lost to him. It had taken all my willpower to push away from him to stop us from ending up sleeping together, but in the back of my mind, I kept wondering how long that would last? It hadn't helped much with Poseidon even after I'd pushed him away. Maybe I should have stayed clear from all of them and I wouldn't be in this situation. Or was I overthinking everything and should just embrace having multiple men in my life. The gods shared after all, right?

I really needed to talk to someone about this. I longed for my best friend. Having girl talk. Now Catina and I were arguing, I didn't have any women in my life to remind me of the things that were really important.

We hadn't spoken in more than a week. Maybe it was time for me to get up off my ass, swallow my pride, and make up with her. I couldn't just let a friendship this strong go down the drain because my personal life had gotten complicated.

As a freelancer, I worked on Saturdays, but Catina would be at home. So I got dressed, covered up my bruises with makeup as much as I could, and drove to Catina's place. Nerves danced in my stomach, but I was foolish to let an argument split up our friendship.

When she opened the front door to her apartment, her eyes widened with shock, her mouth hung open.

"What happened to you?" she asked, genuine concern behind her gaze, and I adored when she worried about me.

"Oh, it's nothing."

She let out a long exhale and gripped her hips. "I can see you're covering it up with makeup."

I shrugged. I hadn't done a great job. "It's from training. I'm using a new weapon, and I'm not very good with it yet." Lies, but they were plausible.

Catina nodded, satisfied for now, though she still eyed me suspiciously.

"I miss you," I said, going for honesty upfront.

Catina's face crumpled, her shoulders curling forward. "I miss you too. I hate that we're fighting."

"I'm sorry for being a bitch," I said, my throat thickening with emotions because just speaking to her again brought back the joy I'd lost since our argument.

"Me too." Catina smiled, and that gave me hope of fixing our relationship.

I stepped into her apartment and hugged her, and we held each other tightly for a long moment, and it was clear she'd been as affected as me. When she let go, she invited me in for coffee, and I followed her to the kitchen.

"How have you been?" she asked.

I shrugged and ran a hand through my loose hair. "I've been better." A hell of a lot better, in fact. This battle with X was really draining me and I didn't know which way to turn with the gods. But I couldn't exactly tell her that.

"How's your man doing?"

"He's okay," I replied, not sure I wanted to open that can of worms yet.

Catina eyed me. "You don't have to hide it all because I was a bitch to you," she said. "I know you don't always see things the same way I do."

I took a deep breath. "We do have different values. I've realized that and I shouldn't have overreacted before."

She smiled that easy smirk that had me relaxing. "So, tell me. What's been happening?"

I leaned a hip against the kitchen counter, watching her make coffee while I told her about Poseidon. I told her her his name was Phil, and met through my trainer. A pathetic name for a god like Poseidon, but I couldn't say who he really was. I hadn't heard of one person naming their kid Poseidon, so using his real name wouldn't work.

"What are you going to do?" she asked. One of her manicured eyebrows arching as she spoke.

We each took a mug and strolled into her living room. I tucked my feet underneath me on the couch and sipped the nutty coffee.

"I know it's complicated, but I'm considering dating him," I finally said, holding the cup close to my chest, watching for my friend's reaction.

She tilted her head slightly, and blinked a bit faster than usual. "So, you're dumping Al?"

Al? Right, the name I had given her instead of telling her it was Apollo. Al and Phil. God, it sounded like the start of a bad joke.

I shook my head. "No, I'm not dumping him."

Catina narrowed her eyes at me. "You want to date both of them?"

I froze, feeling as if we'd already had this discussion the last time we talked. "It's unlike anything else I've experienced. They each make me feel like I'm floating on clouds. They're both different, but they fit with me so perfectly."

"How is this okay?" Catina asked. "Who are you?"

I looked at her in surprise, unsure if I'd heard her right. "What do you mean?"

"I've never known this side of you. I thought we were on the same page when it came down to guys. We've always talked about true love and dating and all that shit, and you've never told me you're fine screwing two guys at once."

Oh, if only she knew the truth… I didn't like the harshness of her tone but didn't want to jump the gun again. The whole concept of being with more than one guy was new. I struggled with it, so who was I to judge Catina so quickly if she fought to accept it? I took a deep breath and calmed myself. "I guess it never came up. I've never met more than one guy whom I've liked. This is a first for me too."

"And now, suddenly, there're two," Catina said flatly.

I nodded. I'd intended to ask her advice, to tell her about Hades and what would happen between the two brothers. But she was already struggling to swallow the idea of me dating two guys. I wasn't going to add more to the mix.

"Look, Elyse, I know they're hot. I have no idea where you find these guys in all honesty because I never seen anyone who looks like Phil in my life. He's like a god."

Bingo.

"But just because they're easy on the eyes doesn't mean you should date them both. They're probably assholes."

If only they were. Even then, it might not put me off. Hades was a total asshole, and I couldn't stay away from him, either. I didn't know what it was, but I desired him just as much as the rest of them and when he left me without looking back, it nailed me in the gut every time.

"They're actually really nice," I said. "Both of them. That's why I can't be with just one"

Catina shook her head and looked down at the coffee in her cup. What was she thinking? That I was asking for trouble? That I ought to select one guy because that was the norm society expected from me? But when did I ever follow the social protocol for anything I did?

Catina glanced up at me, the bridge of her nose pinched and her lips thinning. “I don’t know how you can do this. It’s totally immoral.”

I sighed. *Here we go again.* But I wanted her to understand this went deeper than me just desiring two handsome men.

She sighed and raised her chin in a defiant manner. “I know we don’t have the same morals. I’m beginning to get that. But it just… gets me. I’m struggling to look past this.”

“I see that,” I said softly. “But we’re not doing anything wrong. I’m not marrying them both or anything.”

“I’m not talking about the law,” she said.

I squared my shoulders, and a fire ignited in my chest at her implied accusations. “What am I supposed to do? I like them both. I’m not going to give either of them up.”

I’d wondered about not dating Poseidon, but now Catina was telling me what to do and who to be, I almost had to date him long-term just to show her I could do whatever I wanted. If it ever came down to giving up one of the men in my life, it might very well tear out a piece of my heart. God, I sounded so dramatic.

Nope, that wasn’t childish at all.

"I'm sorry, Elyse. I can't do this. I'm not going to stand by and watch you whore yourself out." Her words were like hand grenades, and they damn stung like a bomb going off.

I gaped at her, shocked she would say something like that. "Excuse me?"

"It's wrong!"

"Did you just call me a whore?" I asked.

"Not like that." Her cheeks blanched. "But you can't fuck around like this."

I stood, nearly spilling the coffee I hadn't even drunk. "I'll do whatever I want. I thought we were okay with this."

"Where will you draw the line? Three, four, five men?" She looked up at me, holding my stare.

I couldn't answer her because I'd never thought about drawing a line. This was about following my feelings. About giving in to the power I felt, the attraction I couldn't explain to anyone. How incredible the men made me feel, giving me more purpose to life than just fighting and training. They made me feel whole again and not so alone in a world without any family. I loathed the moments when I felt so alone I cried myself to sleep because I missed my dad and brothers and mom so much.

I wasn't one of the gods, but I was inexplicably pulled to them in a way I'd never been drawn to anyone, and I just didn't believe in dating one person. I didn't see the point.

And if I lost friends along the way because of my decision, so be it then. I wasn't like the rest of the human race anyway. I'd never fit in, and I was sick and tired of having this argument.

"Coming here was a mistake." I put my cup on the table and marched toward the door, hating that I thought I could somehow make our friendship work again.

"You're walking out on me?" Catina asked.

I halted and faced her. "You walked out on me the last time, remember? Are only you allowed to do that?"

"I thought you were here to apologize." She sounded upset, as if she wasn't battling anymore, like she wanted to cry. But I wasn't in the mood for this shit. I was furious about the accusations when I already faced so much shit in my life. I just wanted someone who accepted me for who and what I was. No judgment. If she didn't want us to fight again, she shouldn't have been a bitch.

"I thought you were willing to accept who I am," I said, turning to the door. I opened it and closed it again behind me, not slamming it like I so desperately wanted to. Who said I couldn't control myself when I was pissed off?

I climbed into my car and drove off. I was so mad. Tears rolled over my cheeks. Catina and I were just not going to see eye to eye on this. It really was over, and that shattered me.

CHAPTER 18

Apollo

I didn't visit Elyse nearly as much as I desired to and that was bullshit. But I couldn't taunt Zeus with a relationship that was forbidden. Except I was falling hard for Elyse, and I was willing to sacrifice being on Earth for her, but if I was banished from here, I'd never see her again anyway.

It had been a long time since being with anyone made me feel so alive. There was a whole world of splendor to show her. I yearned to take her to every corner of Earth and spoil her. Something about seeing her smiling, her eyes glistening with excitement, filled me with joy. So, me being self-sacrificing wasn't exactly going to help either of us if Zeus got involved, which meant playing it safe a while longer, at least until the current shit with X ended. Then I'd work on trying to convince Zeus to change his mind about me dating mortals.

While Poseidon was in town, I hung low. I saw Elyse when I could, but Poseidon and Hades were all over the show with X being a dick and I didn't want to draw unnecessary attention to myself. But with X around, the negativity fought my energy to brighten the sun beyond the gloomy clouds coating the city of Chicago. What we needed was to work as a team to defeat X, and that was if the three other gods on Earth could stop bickering long enough to do so.

There was too much darkness out there lately.

I got on my bike, ready to go visit Elyse. I missed holding her, talking to her, spending time with her.

On the way to her place, anger rode on my skin, clawing its raging hands down my back. The power wasn't mine, but someone else's. I turned right onto the next road, following the energy, curious what expelled such energy. Someone was royally pissed off, and it lured me to them because it seemed all wrong, though it wasn't X. His power held a hardness to it, but this was different.

When I parked the bike, Ares stood in the middle of the quiet road lined with warehouses in an industrial part of the city. He radiated anger in shock waves. He only partially seemed like himself, his body bigger, his muscles bulging, his eyes a strange red. He was shifting into another form that personified his rage better than his normal body did. The anger fractured the road around him, hairline cracks that fanned out like spiderwebs. It ran up the buildings, too. It wouldn't collapse anything, but in time, there would be structural issues if he carried on like this.

I got off my bike. "Hey, man, what's going on?" I asked, strolling over to him.

"None of your fucking business," Ares barked.

"Hey, calm down. This isn't my fault."

"Sure," Ares said. "Bet you never called me a coward behind my back, huh?"

I couldn't answer that because I had. Not recently, but when you were immortal, it all counted from day one. And what it came down to was that Ares did things for himself, what made him happy, leaving others in danger if it meant getting what he wanted. Or at least that was how it had been so long ago. But everyone changed, right? *Look at me living amongst the humans and falling for a mortal.*

"I'm sick and tired of being seen as the weak one when I'm the one willing to go to war. And now I'm called down here, but that's not good enough, either. It's bullshit if you ask me. Of course no one fucking asks me. But I can take on X."

The more he ranted, the worse his anger grew. His body bulged and he looked as if he'd explode. He was probably transforming into a creature or animal.

"Easy, Ares." I held out my hand with my palms down, as if I were trying to calm a wild animal. Which

Ares was at this point. He'd lose his shit if he kept going this way. And sometimes even when he didn't want to. Let's face it, he wasn't the king of self-control.

"Don't tell me to calm down!" he shouted. "I'm so over everyone instructing me on who I have to be!"

I sighed, well aware of how fucked-up that felt. I'd been there with Zeus ordering me to be his entertainment up in Olympus. To not fall for any mortals.

"What's going on here?" Elyse asked, striding into the road from a side street. My stomach flipped, like it always did when I saw her. But she looked like shit. Black eye, bruised. Scratches and marks on her arms and neck. My chest caught on fire with the urge to destroy anyone who'd done this to her.

"What happened to you?" I reached out to her.

"Yeah, ask her. She'll explain to you how I fucked it all up for her," Ares spat the words with venom.

Elyse shook her head. "Don't make this about you, Ares."

He snorted. "And there we have it. Ares is the issue again."

I shook my head. He was out of control, furious about something and causing way too much trouble. It wasn't necessary for him to be this ridiculous about everything. Even if he was angry, which we all had a right to be.

"Yeah, actually, you are," Elyse said. "What did I say? Have my back. Work with me. It would have all gone differently if you'd listened to me."

“I fought. That’s what I’m here for.”

I’d been aware there had been a fight. The magic the combat threw off had been insane. But I hadn’t reached them before the battle stopped, and lately teleporting had me popping all over the place as if my energy had gone haywire when I traveled in Chicago. It didn’t send me where I needed to be.

Elyse glared at Ares—he must have done something real fucked-up. My chest tightened at seeing her hurt and always finding herself in the middle of trouble and fights. That worried me the most. She’d been in pain, and she seemed on edge, her body tense, her lips thin. She deserved a break from all this shit.

“Are you okay?” I asked, reaching for Elyse once again.

“I will be as soon as X is taken care of.” She sounded as if she were wilting.

I closed the distance between us and drew her into my arms. She sagged against me a little, and I kissed the top of her head.

“This is great, a cute little reunion,” Ares said bitterly. “Don’t mind me. I’m just the third wheel.”

“Fuck, you’re sour,” I said. Ares was really shitty today.

“Yeah, well, you’re the one who joined my party. I didn’t look you up.”

I sighed. My arms were still around Elyse. I wasn’t going to let go of her until I had a reason to. The temptation to whisk us both away, maybe somewhere across the planet, was tempting, but she wasn't the kind to leave unresolved problems behind. And I couldn't do that to her.

"Oh, this is fun," Hades snarled, stepping out of the shadows of several trees across the road. He strolled toward us, eyes hooded by shadows, arms tight by his side.

Fuck. As if we needed him to join us.

"What do you want?" Ares growled in Hades's direction.

"I have a bone to pick with Elyse."

"Yeah?" Ares asked with a chuckle. "Get in line."

"What the fuck is going on here?" I demanded.

Elyse sighed and stepped away from me. I hated that she had, but I guessed if they were all pitted against her, she wanted to stand on her own two feet. The last thing she'd ever be was a damsel in distress. I stepped behind her.

"So, who's going first?" Hades asked, rubbing his hands together. He was like a child, excited about what was to come. Except it was probably going to be a fight because Ares was pissed off and Hades was a dick. Standard. Nothing new when it came to those two.

"You can go," Ares said with a sweep of his hand. "I'm already the odd one out here."

Hades shrugged. "Fine." He looked at Elyse. They were really putting her on the spot. "I want answers about where we stand. That's why we're all here, isn't it?"

He looked at me, then Ares. What the fuck was he talking about? I looked at Elyse. She was staring at her feet. I frowned at Hades.

"Can we not do this right now?" She looked exhausted. Physically and emotionally, her voice wavering.

"Then when?" Hades asked. "Are you going to finish this off with them? Who's first? Ares?"

Ares shook his head. "Forget it, man. You can have her. I'm out."

"Hey, now," I said, immediately pissed. No one could just "have" her. She was mine.

Ares didn't bother to respond. He disappeared in a cloud of rage, leaving us with the damage he'd started.

Swell guy.

Hades stormed toward us.

"So now that we're down to the two of us, are you going to man up and do this, or what?" he asked.

"Fuck you, Hades," Elyse spat. "Don't talk to me about manning up until you can learn how to be a real man. For a god, you're pretty pathetic when it comes to standing up and doing the right thing."

She turned around and marched away.

"Seriously?" he said. "All of this happens, three guys stand together, and I end up being the one gets rejected?"

Elyse didn't respond. I didn't, either. I had nothing to say to him. I'd suspected that he had had a thing with Elyse. Judging by the rejection she'd just thrown into his face, that wasn't an ongoing thing. But no one held on to Hades for long. Not even Persephone.

I would have said something about it, but that would have been a low blow and I was too busy running after Elyse to wound Hades.

When I caught up to her, she had tears running down her cheeks.

"Ignore them," I offered.

"It's not that easy." Her next breath hiccupped.

When I glanced over my shoulder, Hades had disappeared. Good riddance. Everywhere he went, he caused chaos.

"I know," I said. She'd been telling me what was going on. Not with Hades and Ares; I had to admit I was mostly in the dark about that. I'd sort of assumed I was the only one in her life, so knowing that wasn't the case was a bit of a jab in my heart. But it was normal for gods to love more than one person, and she was as far removed from the humans and their way of thinking as we were.

So I had to get over my colossal ego and accept that Elyse had the right to love whomever she wanted.

As long as she loved me, too.

That was going to be a fucking bitter pill to swallow. I would deal with that. Just not now. She needed me.

I grasped her wrist as she was still marching down the sidewalk and drew her back to me. She looked at me with eyes so raw, I yearned to stop all of this and make the pain go away.

"Sometimes I wish I were just a human," she said. She leaned her forehead against my chest, and I put my hand on her back. "Sometimes, I wish I had nothing to do with all of this."

That hurt, and my stomach tensed with pain. It would mean that she'd live a life without me too. But it wasn't fair of me to dwell on that.

"We'll figure it out, okay?" I said.

She nodded against me, but I sensed her disbelief, her need to let go of everything going on around her, her wish it was all just a bad dream.

Even if that included me.

All I could do was be there for her. So that was what I did.

CHAPTER 19

Hades

When Ares ghosted away like the coward he was, I only stuck around long enough for Elyse to give me the cold shoulder again. I should have known that was going to happen, but I hoped that the group setting would put more pressure on her to admit whether she did or didn't want to be with me.

No go. She was adamant to put me in my place, and I hated to admit it had worked. I felt two inches tall now she'd rejected me. As if I weren't used to that already. But it still stung.

When I left, I didn't go back to my shitty dump of a house. I went after Ares to find him. The guy was full of shit on a good day. On bad days, he was impossible. But he was angry about something and I wanted to know what was going on with him. Didn't need another loose cannon in the city.

And I was willing to bet Elyse affected him too.

"What's grating your tits?" I asked when I'd tracked him down to a deserted pier that led out onto Lake Michigan.

"What do you care?" Ares kicked a loose stone.

He sat down on the dock. The wood had silvered, and the water was choppy with the wind. The sky was gray, but when wasn't it these days?

"Come on. We're all furious about something. Personally, I don't like being fucked around by women. What about you?"

Ares glanced at me. "Are you here to start something? Because I'm not in the mood."

I shook my head. "Just looking for companionship, my friend."

"Not your friend," he said, raising his eyebrows. "But if you must know, the gods think I'm a coward, and that makes me furious because I'm actually doing something about this shit with X. Which is your fault, so I don't know why you're even here."

I was immediately irritated, fire slicing through me. So, everyone was blaming me for this, then. That was just fucking dandy. But that was beside the point. Guessed we all held preconceived notions about each other.

"Usually the accusations don't bug me." Ares carried

on as if he didn't mind that I was here, even though he kept questioning my presence.

We all needed a shoulder to cry on. That I was the shoulder for Ares was annoying, but there it was. I itched for a fight and just waiting for the juice to do it. If anyone would give me a good fight, it was the god of war himself. He could help me shake off the frustration building within me.

"So why does it bug you now?" I asked, crouching nearby.

"Thanks for not telling me you disagree with the rest of them," he responded sarcastically.

I straightened my spine. I wasn't going to say words if I didn't mean them.

"So?" I prompted.

Ares sighed. "It bugs me because Elyse seems to agree with you about how she sees me and that really pisses me off. And I'm pretty sure you know how shitty it is to get rejected by her."

I frowned. "You got rejected by Elyse?"

Ares nodded. "Yep, we kissed, and she shoved me aside. But what are you going to do, right?"

I suddenly saw red because here I longed to be with her, and yet Ares had made a move on her. Sure, she rejected him. And yeah, gods were known for sharing partners, but it was the fact Elyse wasn't accepting me, and how she continuously pushed me away. That was what pissed me off. I couldn't even control my anger, it rose so quickly through me, burning me up on the inside. I tried to swallow it, but there was too much rage.

Ares glanced over at me as I stood. "What the fuck, man?"

I shook my head. I was going to kill this guy if I stayed because I needed to unleash my anger. So, I focused on keeping calm enough to breathe and got the hell out of there before I did something that would really cause trouble. This was no longer a fight I was looking for. I marched out of there.

When I finally found Elyse, she was at the training center, and she was alone. Good. I wasn't going to let up just because Apollo might have been around. Heracles had to have been here somewhere, yet I couldn't sense either of them, and that was good enough for me. This was between the two of us. She and I had fucked here before, but this time, I was burning with anger.

"What the hell is your problem?" I demanded.

We were in front of the training center—she hadn't even made it inside yet.

"Excuse me?" she asked, one of her brows arching as she turned around to face me. Most people were scared of me, but her anger rose to meet mine the moment I charged at her.

"Apollo and my brother aren't enough; you are now getting with Ares, too."

"I didn't do anything," she said defiantly, lifting her chin.

Right, he'd said she'd rejected him. Just as she'd

done to me, and I wanted to understand why she still gave me mixed signals. And why I wasn't good enough for her. I narrowed my eyes at her. "But you want to, don't you?"

"Since when do you give a shit about what I want?" Elyse asked. "All you care about is yourself, anyway."

That was totally beside the point. And not completely true. I'd just learned that it was the safest way to ensure I didn't get fucked over.

"When are you going to be straightforward with me?" I asked.

"When you fucking deserve it!" Elyse shouted, her arms stiff by her side.

"And who are you to decide my worth?"

"You decided mine. Right from the very start, you decided I'm not worth sticking around for unless you want to get your rocks off. And I'm stupid enough to fall for it every time." Despite her defiant expression, the hurt in her eyes told a different story.

And this mixed messaging messed me up. I just needed to know what she wanted.

"That's not fair," I said.

"No? What's fair? Leaving me in the police station? Here? Treating me like a piece of ass?"

That wasn't how I saw her. I'd been a dick, but I'd tried to stop myself from getting hurt. Hurting her had been a byproduct, and in hindsight, I saw that now, loathed myself for my behavior. Since arriving on Earth, she'd crawled into my heart like no other and I didn't know how to respond when I didn't want to get my heart ripped out again. But I'd made things so much fucking worse.

"I'm not doing this," she said, shaking her head and turning around.

"Don't you walk away from me," I said, grabbing her arm so she wouldn't leave.

She spun around and swung a fist at me. It came so fast, I couldn't dodge her punch, and she struck me square in the nose.

"Fuck!" I shouted, letting her go. But I'd engaged. I'd started this fight. And Elyse wasn't going to back down. I knew her better than that.

We fell into our normal routine. If we weren't fucking, we were fighting. And I'd take our combat over not being with her.

She was stronger this time. It was a normal hand-to-hand bout, no weapons. But she hit me with a force she hadn't before. When she planted a kick in my side, she nearly winded me. That wasn't easy to do. My palm slammed into her ribs, and she doubled over in pain. She had a wound there or something.

For a moment, I felt sorry for her. I didn't want to hurt her. But she retaliated, raining punches on my face, and I had to do something to stop her. So I shoved her backward. She blocked my strikes and grimaced in pain, her face twisting, and the reaction stopped the blows.

We took it to the ground outside the center. She

pinned me to the asphalt. I kicked out and returned the favor. I yanked her braid. She screamed in anger and placed a well-aimed kick between my legs. It was a dirty move I hadn't seen coming.

Good thing I had balls of steel. Not literally. I could handle the agony, even though threads of pain jolted through me every now and then. Hell, she was strong.

I hit Elyse on her side another time, and blood seeped into her shirt. She was angry and aching, sneering in agony and frustration when she attacked yet again.

"Just stop," I said.

She didn't seem to hear me, and her blows grew sluggish. Her energy levels were depleting. I had a feeling whatever battle she'd gotten into had taken a lot more out of her than I'd thought. We had to stop.

Again, she attacked me. She punched me so hard in my stomach, I curled around her fist, and she kneed me in the ribs. I wasn't injured, so much as stunned. I grabbed her leg, yanking her off balance. I wrapped her braid around my hands like I had done so many times while we fucked, and I leaned my knee on her chest. She cried out in pain.

"Stop this!" I shouted down at her. "You're not going to get free. Let's just talk."

"I'll never stop standing up for myself," she gritted out.

Her dark eyes challenged me. Her makeup had rubbed off and I realized how bad she looked. I felt a pang of guilt for being this hard on her. "Or are you going to kill me again?" She was so irate; her words scalded on my skin. "You've done it before. Just do it again; you know you're low enough to do it."

Fuck her. She was such a stunning person and in her fury she was beautiful. I couldn't let her up. I wasn't going to concede. My pride was a bitch, but it was in control. I had to stop her from going berserk.

And I wasn't going to kill her, either.

She threw a fist under my chin, catching me off-guard, as I'd been focusing on her eyes, trying to make her see we had to do things differently. I reeled off her. She scrambled up and charged me.

Up on my feet, I blocked her assault, but my fury bated. She struck me right in the neck with a slicing punch, choking me as the heel of my foot caught on a rock. I was losing balance. Instinct took over. I swung a fist out to block hers, but she shifted, and my fist slid past her defenses.

My punch slammed into her face so hard, I almost saw stars for her sake. And her eyes rolled back, and she fell backward. My heart dropped. I crashed to the ground backward from my momentum but scrambled to her side.

"Elyse!"

She lay there unconscious, and my blood ran cold.

I fell to my knees next to her and cradled her head, my chest splintering. Guilt seared my mind. If I hadn't already hated myself before, I loathed myself now. We should have ended our battle, I should have walked away, she should have ended her attacks. None of that stopped the blade twisting in my heart when all I longed for was to hold her in my arms, to make her laugh, to pleasure her. To bring her whatever she desired.

But I'd fucked up everything. From the beginning, I'd made every mistake possible with Elyse, trying to protect my feelings while I'd fallen so damn hard for her, not realizing until it was too late. Now we just couldn't seem to move past this fighting stage. I'd never intended to hurt her.

Fuck!

I used to believe I was in love with Persephone, but after discovering it was a spell, a trick, I'd been pissed with everyone. I never wanted love again. Yet Elyse was intoxicating and addictive. She'd swept into my heart so fast, I'd stood no chance.

Looking down at her bruised face, her delicate features and her swollen lips, my chest squeezed tightly.

Maybe she was right not to love me back when all I caused her was agony. She bled from a gash on her lip and another deeper one on her forearm. I would tend to her wounds, keep her safe, do what the fuck I was meant to do from the moment I'd met her.

Standing with her in my arms, I turned and carried her away.

CHAPTER 20

Elyse

When I opened my eyes, I was staring at my white bedroom ceiling. My head pounded terribly, the ache thumping across my temples. I was too scared to turn my head and couldn't see properly out of one eye. A sharp pain in my side made me feel as if I had been stabbed.

"Elyse," Heracles said, his voice reverberating in my head, his face coming into view. His eyes held the same kind of gentle concern my dad had displayed each time I hurt myself during training. Heracles's bronze hair had been pulled back into a ponytail and he wore a leather strap around his head, the one that told me he had been to Mount Olympus to see his father. "How are you feeling?"

"Sore," I croaked, then swallowed hard. My throat felt like sandpaper.

"Here," Heracles said, handing me a bottle of water.

"What happened?" I asked, trying to wrack my brain to remember how I'd gotten home but coming up short.

"I don't know," Heracles said. "I was going to ask you that. I hadn't heard from you when I turned up at the training center, and you didn't answer your phone. So, I came over to find your door unlocked and you on the bed looking as if X had regurgitated you and spat you out. But someone looked after you. You have fresh bandages on your injuries."

Flashes of Hades came to me. Our fight. His fist to my face, then my world blackened. My heart sank. Why would he care for me if he was willing to hurt me like this? He hadn't killed me. And I'd fought him. I hadn't stopped when I could have. When he'd begged me to end the fight. But I was so angry at everything—at him, at my life.

This was as much my fault as his. I'd pushed too far.

"What happened? Can you remember?" Heracles asked, his brow creasing.

I wanted to shake my head but caught myself. "No," I lied.

I wasn't going to tell him that Hades had done this. I didn't want him to look like a bad guy. We had a love-hate relationship, and I'd pushed him to get on the receiving end of this much hate. I should have known it would go this far. I should never have engaged in this state.

"This has to stop," Heracles said. "X has to be stopped."

He still thought my injuries had been the result of Hades's deadly shadow. The truth wasn't far from it, so I'd leave him to think that was the case.

I pushed myself so I could sit up. My chest felt as if my ribs were being ripped apart, and I groaned from the stabbing across my middle, but I managed.

"What's going on with you lately?" Heracles asked. "You've skipped training, you're distracted—it feels like every time I turn my back, you get into some kind of trouble. This is unlike you."

I squared my shoulders and regretted the move. Every inch of my body was stiff and screamed with pain. But I'd canceled a couple of times only, like the time I'd gone away with Apollo to France and we'd arrived home late.

"Look," Heracles continued. "I know you're having issues with the gods. You can talk to me, you know. You don't have to do everything alone."

I sighed. How was I going to be able to tell him what I felt? That Apollo and Poseidon were right up there in the "getting serious" category and that Hades, with all the shit he did to me, wasn't very far behind? That Ares was inching closer, too, which was insane. I didn't understand the emotions myself, but I couldn't ignore those four men who were in my thoughts daily.

The lure between us grew stronger with each passing moment, yet I just couldn't find the balance of making it all smooth when they seemed to react with fury when they saw me with one of the others. What the fuck was I meant to do?

When I didn't say anything, Heracles nodded. "It's okay. You don't have to talk if you don't want to. I can guess. My uncles are both in town, and they have reputations with women. And Apollo is a hell of a catch. I've heard it from a lot of mortals over the centuries."

"You make it sound like I'm just whoring myself out." Catina's words came back to me, and I cringed that I'd repeated her accusation out loud.

"No." Heracles shook his head, his expression serious, his eyes like round discs. "That's not what this is at all. And I'm sad that you see it that way. You might not be able to help who you love, but that doesn't mean that you shouldn't love them."

When I didn't answer and glanced down at my hands, the scratches and bruises on my arms, he added, "All of them."

I looked up at him.

He leaned against the wall near the window and folded his arms. The guy was handsome, and I hoped he found someone to be with him one day. If I didn't have a shit load of problems, I might even pick his brain about where he'd been the other night and discover if indeed he'd found someone.

"You're fighting yourself so hard over this that

there's no energy left to fight X," he said. "Don't think I don't see what's going on."

As tempting as the idea of hiding under the blanket right now was—at the realization he was witnessing me clumsily trying to push through life—I met his gaze. "What am I supposed to do? I don't know who I am anymore." Maybe the old me might have followed Catina's morals and only had one guy, but I wasn't sure. I just felt different now.

"Be who this situation molds you to be. Embrace and accept what you're becoming. The gods love very deeply, but they don't love exclusively. And you're a lot more like us than you are like the humans."

"How is that possible?" I asked. "How can I not be like the humans when I am one?"

"Maybe that's not all human blood in your system," he said.

I frowned, staring at him as he smiled. "What does that mean?"

He hesitated. "All I'm saying is that the power that comes with what Zeus gave you doesn't originate from nothing."

That didn't make sense, either. Was he implying Zeus's blessing on my family did more than make us strong, that it had changed us?

"You're not wrong to feel what you're sensing. Don't fight the change. It's putting you at a disadvantage, distracting you from what's really happening."

He made sense. My battered body and torn

emotions were proof. I'd gotten hurt more often because of how I felt for the gods than because of my fights with X. They drove me insane, and I'd been battling my attractions, letting the expectations of mortals like Catina dictate how I should behave. Even with that thought, putting my desires into action was a whole different ball game.

"I'm losing myself, Herc," I said, terrified of what I'd become, that I'd never feel human again.

Would I withdraw from society to just fight monsters and gods for eternity? Live amongst mortals and feel alone and distant—just like the gods who were on Earth? Not really belonging but taking and doing what they liked? Dad told me to hold on to a simple life, to not forget where I'd come from, that the lure to believe I was above others was overwhelming. Was the sensation coursing through my veins what Dad had referred to?

"You're still finding yourself," Heracles added, drawing me out of my thoughts.

"No," I said. "Everything about me is changing. I used to be someone I could still see my parents in. I could still relate to Catina, my best friend. Now? There's nothing left of the girl my parents raised. And I've lost Catina completely. What is there left for me if I don't fit in this world? I have nowhere to go if I'm not the person I thought I was."

Heracles sighed. "You'll figure it out, Elyse. I promise."

I shook my head because I wasn't so sure.

Heracles looked at the clock on my bedside table. "I have to go," he said. "Call me if you need me. And don't leave the apartment, okay? You can't afford to get into a fight now. You won't make it, and it's your job to spare your lives as much as you can."

"Okay," I said. With each passing day, Heracles reminded me more and more of my dad. Dishing out instructions and leaving me to my own devices.

He nodded and left the apartment.

"I'm telling your friend next door to check in on you, just in case, okay?" he called out.

Oliver? Great. Maybe seeing him wouldn't be so bad. At least it was a connection to my old life that hadn't burned out yet.

When Heracles left, I shifted down on the bed so I lay down again. Exhaustion swept through me.

I closed my eyes, but sleep wouldn't come. Images of my parents flashed before me. I remembered how it used to be around the dinner table, joking and laughing, talking about our training that day, what we'd learned when we sparred against each other.

I missed the warmth that came with that, the sense of belonging. Even though we hadn't fit into this world, we'd still had each other.

Now? Now I was by myself. There was no one else left like me and I was so fucking alone. I used to think of loneliness as something that would pass, leave me after I made more friends, socialized. Except the feeling stayed with me, as if it were part of my DNA.

I adored the guys, even if they pissed me off, but I didn't fit in with them. And I was becoming more and more removed from the humans. It terrified me to sit between two worlds, belonging to neither. I had lost a part of myself when I had died the first time, a part that I hadn't realized I'd cared so much about until it was gone.

Wasn't that always the way?

I was losing my connection to the humans and that scared me because I realized I was truly, completely on my own. I'd been born into a life of responsibility, to stand up for the humans who couldn't stand up for themselves. The job was a burden, but I'd carried the tasks with pride because they defined who I was. Yet I was still connected to the world around me.

All that was left was what I could do for others. I had nothing for myself, nothing I could say belonged to me and me alone.

And that was pretty horrible shit. Because I wished I still had something. Anything.

I rolled onto my side and tried to get comfortable. No matter how I tried, I was still in pain. If only Hades had killed me—I would have lost a life, but I would have healed fully, and I'd have been in so much agony now.

But I would have been even further removed from the humans. Not that it would have made such a big difference. I'd already lost my connection to them. I was already on my own.

The upside about dying was I would have become stronger again. Strong enough to handle X and take him out once and for all.

I closed my eyes and took a deep breath, trying to will myself into sleep.

"Elyse." The voice floated through my head, and I rolled over, falling back into slumber. But when the male voice came again, stronger, my eyes shot open. I jerked upward, sitting in bed, searching the room. But no one was there, only me.

Heavy laughter rang in my ears, and I turned too fast to check behind me, but my ribs screamed with pain. I cringed, holding my breath until the ache passed. I couldn't move fast.

"You'll die today," he screeched.

That time, I recognized the voice ringing in my head. It was the bastard, X.

Ice coursed through my veins that he'd come back for me when I was alone and injured. I shuffled out of bed, pushing my legs out from under the sheet, and stood, scanning the room for any sign of him appearing. I hurt everywhere from my pinkie to my ears.

"Show yourself," I snarled, limping toward my

closet where I kept a couple of long blades. "Why are you just threatening me? You scared?"

A deep grumble rolled through my mind once more, and I stumbled into the closet door. "Give yourself willingly to me. I can make it hurt less. Either way, your time will end with me. I'm thinking today is a good day for you to die."

"Fuck off!"

I ripped open the closet as my skin rippled with goosebumps, and I felt him stand behind me before I looked around. Reaching in past my coats, I grabbed a knife and turned to find the prick across the room from me. Tall, dark, and gaunt. His body almost shimmered in and out of existence. I couldn't see his face, as it seemed like a pool of darkness.

A sting shot across my ribs, and I grimaced from the excruciating ache of twisting around. How the hell would I battle X in this condition? He'd win, take me, and no one would be the wiser of what had become of me.

Sweat rolled down my spine and facing death, when I knew I didn't stand a chance against him, terrified me. Was this how his victims felt as they realized he'd kill them?

Heaviness pressed in around me. The air choked me, and I gripped the hilt of the blade tight. Despite the fear gathering in my chest, a fiery rage also rose through me that this fucker would come for me when I was at my lowest. I'd survived all these years on my own, fighting all kinds of monsters, and now even gods, so I refused to back down. But I also wasn't a fool who thought I could win this battle. Last time I faced off against him, I'd barely survived because Poseidon and Ares had come to help. X had gotten stronger, while I was weaker in my state.

He stuck an arm out, a bony hand with long fingers curled to call me to him.

"I'll die before I give myself willingly to you." And a thought occurred to me. Who said I had no way out of this situation? I could take matters into my own hands. I'd already lost so much—I couldn't risk what I had left now.

Either I succumb to death and never come back or be reborn.

The steely resolve that settled inside me was more powerful than anything I'd felt before. I was a Lowe. I was here to look after the humans. I was here to fight X, who'd stepped out of line and killed my people without any right to do so.

And I was the one put on Earth to stop him.

No matter what.

X stepped toward me. "I won't ask again."

So I'd stop him. Do what needed to be done. To protect innocents. I'd take the bastard out because I was sick and tired of him claiming lives that weren't his to keep.

With my back to the closet, I crouched and stuck my hand inside, pushing my boots out of the way. The safe had been installed before I'd moved in. I'd thought it was a waste of time—I never put anything of worth in it, and I used my weapons too often to put them in here.

"Why are you doing this?" I asked, eyeing X as I set my blade down next to my feet.

Familiar with the keypad layout, I put in the code—my dad's birthday—and the heavy door swung open. I took out a matte black box and laid it on the closet floor at my back, then opened it with a shaky hand.

The decision was my choice.

Dad's gun fit perfectly into the sponge around it, bullets packed upright so their tips were razor-sharp at my touch. I'd practiced using it years ago, loading and unloading it in the dark, behind my back, in any condition to survive should the situation arise that I needed such a weapon. The smooth metal was cold against my skin, but the gun was already loaded. Perfectly balanced, not too heavy, and small enough for a woman's hands. It was the ideal weapon—I'd thought so since the moment I first picked it up when my dad was polishing it once.

X lunged toward me, a trail of black fog following him.

A panicked scream strangled my chest.

He seized my throat and lifted me up and off my feet. My air passageway blocked, and my lungs stung. Dread sunk through me like cement. It was a pity these were the circumstances I finally used the weapon under. But I needed strength, and I wouldn't let him take my life.

I smiled at Death and lifted the gun to my mouth.

It was my choice was to be reborn rather than let this monster kill me.

X's laughter flatlined at the sight of the weapon, his free hand striking for my gun.

With a deep inhale, I shoved the gun into my mouth and pulled the trigger.

CHAPTER 21

Elyse

When I opened my eyes, I buzzed all over with adrenaline. The aches were gone, and I was ready to jump up and take on anything. Instead, I lay on my bed, blinking up at my ceiling with a weird case of déjà vu. This time I didn't feel like death warmed me up. I seemed more as if I'd been recharged with some kind of power-up that had left me humming with energy. As if I could run a marathon.

When I sat up, Heracles crouched on the floor with his head in his hands. Apollo stood by the window, his shoulders curled forward.

He saw me first, his eyes widening. "Elyse." He rushed to me.

Heracles looked up, jumped to his feet from the floor, and came to me, too.

They both studied me as if they were sure something would be wrong. Worry had blanched their cheeks, and their breaths came fast. But I didn't sense anything was wrong with me. Apollo was the first to let out a sigh of relief.

When Heracles found nothing wrong, his gaze went from concerned to angry, his brow creasing into a tangle of lines.

"Do you know how much trouble you caused?" His voice shook, as if he hadn't planned on saying that so loud, but it came gushing out anyway.

"I feel great," I said.

"How nice for you," He said sarcastically. "You just about scared the shit out of your neighbor when he came to check on you like I asked him to."

Shit. I had completely forgotten about Oliver, but I also hadn't expected X to pay me a visit. I glanced over at the closet door. It was closed, but a crimson mark peeked out from underneath it, as if the blood that had leaked out of my head hadn't wanted to be contained by secrecy. It amazed me that I could think about that so easily, but I figured it was because I didn't see it as a moment of taking my life, but evolving. Plus, no way would I have let that monster win.

"What did Oliver do?" I asked, convinced I'd scared him for eternity. How could I explain what I'd done? Because to everyone else, aside from me and the gods, it would look as if I'd taken my own life. My stomach ached at the knowledge I'd drawn Oliver into this mess.

"He phoned me, like I asked him to," Heracles explained. "Except he was hysterical and told me you were dead. You can imagine my surprise after I'd told you not to leave the house."

I shook my head. The movement didn't hurt at all as it had earlier, the first time I'd died. Amazing. "I didn't leave the house."

"She's not wrong," Apollo said.

"Shut up, Apollo," Heracles snapped. He turned back to me. "Oliver didn't only call me. He also called nine-one-one. The ambulance arrived, and they carted you out of here after pronouncing you dead at the scene. Do you know what hell I went through to get you out of the morgue?"

I shook my head again, my stomach twisting over itself that I'd caused so much trouble. The plan had been to escape X and wake up stronger. I hadn't thought about anything else going awry. It was a pure survival instinct. But then again, I hadn't expected someone to find me and have a shitfit. At least, not a human. I'd fought for my life with what had been available. I'd forgotten about Oliver. *Hell!*

If any of the gods had found me, they'd have put me on the bed and that would have been the end of it. Nothing would have been wrong. But Oliver had done what humans did when tragedy struck. He didn't know I could come back to life. Humans usually didn't.

"I guess that's a lot of paperwork? Shit, I didn't want Oliver to find me like that." I cringed on the inside. In hindsight, I should have given it more thought, but it wasn't as if I could tell X to hold his horses before attempting to kill me while I locked the front door.

"You could say so." Apollo sniffed, his attention never leaving me, as if he still couldn't believe what he was looking at. "I had to find all the paperwork that declared you deceased, so your house and job didn't get taken away."

"That was the easy part," Heracles said. "I had to scrub all the humans' memories who'd seen you and knew what it meant. The medical personnel didn't give a shit—humans compartmentalize—but that little friend of yours is traumatized now with no idea why he feels that way."

I took a deep breath and let it out. *Fuck.* "It shouldn't have been this complicated."

"Yeah, hindsight is twenty-twenty," Heracles bit out.

I straightened my shoulders and raised myself to a sitting position. There wasn't much I could do about it now. Did I regret doing it? Fuck, no. Otherwise, X would have really killed me. I regretted that poor Oliver had found me. At least the damage had been contained.

"What I want to know." Apollo folded his muscular arms over his wide chest, "is why you thought it was okay to sacrifice one of your lives. You can't just kill yourself off as a pick-me-up because you're healing too slowly."

"X came to see me… in my home!" I raised my voice so they would get off my case.

Both men stiffened, and I gave them a rendition of what had gone down, why I'd decided to pull out my gun. Saying it all aloud had me trembling with the memory of my decision, how intensely determined X had been to finish me. And it made the whole situation seem so much more real. I hugged myself. *It was a life-or-death decision, and I made the right choice.*

"Shit!" Apollo clasped my hand in his, staring at me with an expression of shock. "I didn't feel the energy of you two fighting, though, or I'd have rushed over here."

"We didn't fight," I admitted. "He'd come to finish me, and I didn't stand a chance in my injured state, so I made the call to handle the confrontation differently." I raised my chin.

Heracles shook his head. "I know you thought you were doing the right thing, but if you would have just engaged X, the energy would have shot out to us gods to help you."

A fire rushed up my neck and cheeks because he hadn't been there facing Death like I had. Where every inch of me had ached, where I'd struggled to wield my knife. "I did what I felt was right at the time. Everything moved so fast. And I don't regret my decision."

Heracles sighed with that disapproving gesture my dad would use, clearly disagreeing.

As gods, they should have handled this from the beginning or at least jumped in alongside me. It might have ended earlier.

"This is my life. Lives. Whatever. If I want to kill myself to save myself, then I'll do it. I get to come back from death one more time, then the next death after that is final. So, what I do is my call." I was ready to finish this with X, my last chance to do so before I lost everything. I was ready to get this over with.

"Yeah, I get that, but I just wish you'd have given us a chance to come to you. You're not fighting X alone anymore," Heracles snapped back.

"I'm stronger now because of it," I insisted. "I can feel the power that almost burns, there's so much of it."

"And you have no idea how to cope," Heracles continued, the bridge of his nose pinching. "We'll have to start over again with our training."

"Not from scratch," I argued. "I can handle the ability."

The two gods looked at each other with raised brows.

"She has no idea," Apollo said to Heracles.

"None."

"Don't talk about me like I'm not here," I snapped. "I'm not a child, and I didn't do something stupid. I don't care what you think."

"What do you care about?" Heracles snarled.

Apollo shook his head and walked away from me. They were both disappointed. Their reaction didn't make me upset like I'd thought it would. It just pissed me off more. I wasn't here to impress anyone. Although it would have been nice if Apollo at least didn't think badly of me. I wanted him to see me in a good light.

I'd done this because I saw no way out and needed more power to combat X. With nothing to lose—except a life that seemed to be a lot more precious to the gods than I thought—I'd done this to give myself a leg up in this war.

"What time is it?" I asked, realizing for the first time it was dark outside. I hopped down from the bed.

"Almost five," Apollo said.

Monday? Tuesday? I'd lost track. "What day?"

"Wednesday. You were out for five days," Apollo said.

I'd lost more time than I'd thought, and a slow grinding ache settled in my chest. How many innocents had lost their lives during this time?

"Crap. Why was I out for so long?"

"Because there was a hell of a lot of damage to your body after the confrontation with X," Heracles explained. "And then that hole in your head had to heal. Do you think that's easy shit to patch up?" He still glared my way.

I couldn't remember the last time I'd seen Heracles this angry.

"What fight with X?" Apollo asked. "She wasn't too badly injured when I saw her last."

I swallowed hard. The battle with Hades happened after Apollo left so I could go train. I hadn't been planning to tell him about it. He didn't need to know I'd picked a fight I couldn't finish. Or that I'd told Heracles I'd battled X to cover up the fight I had with Hades where he'd knocked me out.

Heracles shook his head, put his one hand on his hip and pinched the bridge on his nose between a thumb and forefinger. "X got a hold of her before he came looking for her at her place," Heracles said.

Apollo frowned, his face as white as snow. "When? I didn't feel anything. Usually, when he's in combat with her, the ripples are incredible."

"I wasn't around," Heracles said. "I was on Mount Olympus."

Apollo pinned me with a stare, and his eyes were icy. He knew something was up, he had to. But he didn't challenge me on it and for that, I was grateful. It wasn't necessary to get into that in front of Heracles, too. The weird back-and-forth we had with the three guys just before Hades had found me at the training center had already caused a strain between Apollo and me.

He'd left me with nothing more than a kiss and a promise that he'd come to see me when things were better.

And now, here we were. Well, my decision hadn't gone exactly as planned. But so little had—at least this one had been in my control.

"You can go," Heracles said to Apollo. "I'll stay here with her."

"Why?" I asked. "I can stay here by myself."

Heracles shook his head. "Oh, no. I'm not leaving you alone."

"I don't mind if Apollo stays." While I appreciated the overprotectiveness, I was still an adult with a life that belonged to me. I wasn't going to let him tell me what to do.

"I'm not going to do something stupid," I said. "I've already gotten what I wanted."

Heracles looked pissed off, his brows bunching up. Again, there was nothing that could be done. I'd killed myself to avoid letting X do it, I had come back to life, and that was it. X was a hell of a lot stronger, but then so was I. Now, I had a better chance against Death. Ironic. My upgame scored me additional points to have a chance to defeat X.

"You can go if you're busy," I said to Heracles when he stayed put, looking like he had been one-upped. "I'm an adult, and I get to make my own choices."

"She's right," Apollo said.

"Don't be a pussy, loverboy," Heracles said.

Apollo's features changed, anger flickering over them. He shot out a fist and clipped Heracles on the jaw. "Don't throw around insults," he snapped.

Heracles rubbed his jawline, glaring off with Apollo, his shoulders raised, and fuck, as if I needed these two to break into rumble.

"Please don't," I pleaded.

Heracles met my gaze, then nodded first and lowered his attention.

Apollo came to me and dropped a kiss on my hair. "This doesn't mean I'm okay with what you did." The last word sounded almost desperate, and he took a seat on the bed next to me, not planning on leaving and I adored that.

I nodded. I was okay now. Zeus wouldn't have blessed us with these abilities if they turned us mad or killed us. That made no sense.

Heracles stood in the room near the window, drumming his fingers against his thighs, stewing about something.

"There's nothing you can say to me," I said to him.

"Yeah, that's what bothers me."

"You act like I don't know what I'm doing." And his unsaid words gutted me. My mentor, the trainer for my whole family line didn't believe I could do my job I'd been training for my entire life.

Heracles sighed, while Apollo said nothing. "I'm starting to worry you don't. You never trained for this shit. We practiced going up against centaurs and griffins and all the other creatures X sent to us. But not Death himself. I don't like to say it, but you're in too deep."

I shook my head. "Not now. Not after I died."

"You don't get it," Heracles said. "Dying doesn't make everything better."

I glared at him. What did he know about what I was doing? Heracles and I had been on the same page for so long, but lately, I was starting to wonder if he knew what I was trying to do. Finish X just as I had been training to do, to do what my dad had called my destiny. Protect humans at any cost, even my own life. And that meant doing what was needed… gaining more strength if required. I appreciated his concern but looking just after myself went against everything I'd been brought up to believe. Or maybe Heracles was still trying to mentor me when I'd shot up past how strong he thought I was supposed to be.

Whatever it was, I wasn't here to be lectured to or told I couldn't do something.

"I'm tired," I said. It was a lie.

Heracles nodded. "I guess I should go. I have a class in a couple of hours and I haven't slept."

"Sorry about that."

He huffed a long exhale. "I'm going to go. I'm not going to ask your human friend to check up on you again. I think he's had about as much as he could handle."

"I don't need a babysitter," I said.

Heracles looked at me with a face that suggested a babysitter was exactly what I needed.

But he wasn't going to say it, and I wasn't going to retaliate. I wanted him to leave already, to be on my own and let everything sink in.

"See you," Apollo added.

Finally, Heracles huffed again and left. I waited for a while, making sure I was completely alone with Apollo. He lifted the blanket I was under and I shuffled over as he climbed in and collected me into his arms. My back pressed against his chest, his warm breath in my hair.

"I'm scared of losing you," he said.

"I'm not going anywhere." I hugged his arm around me, and rested my head against his bicep. "But I can't let more innocents die."

"I know you'll do what you have to. But I'm here for you. Anything you need."

"Thanks." I closed my eyes and his body cocooned mine, drowning in his warmth, reminding me I wasn't as alone as I thought I had been. Apollo truly cared for me, and a joy flooded me. This was the feeling I wanted to remember and hold onto when I felt my world falling apart around me.

When I opened my eyes, Apollo was no longer in my bed. I appreciated him staying with me until I fell asleep.

Sunlight drenched through the window. I climbed out and stood in front of my window, looking out at the city as the sun rose, coloring the grays of the night into the browns and golds that the day brought. Chicago could be beautiful if you looked at it the right way. Everything always seemed so dreary, but there was a lot of beauty left in the world.

I turned to my closet. When I opened the door, the blood stain on the carpet was an ugly brown. I'd have to do something about that when I had the chance. The carpet would need replacing; scrubbing wouldn't be enough. And I didn't want to look at it, as it reminded me of the ugly decision I'd made, and despite putting on a brave face in front of Heracles and Apollo that it hadn't affected me, I wasn't fooling myself.

I'd made the call to save my ass, to not let X win, and to continue protecting innocents. Because that was that my dad would have expected of me. *Just get the job done,* he'd say. *No emotions during a fight.* Yet I was drowning in confused emotions about everything in my life.

Except I refused to dwell on them when I had other things to do. I took out my warrior clothes and my weapons, laying them out on the bed and going through the systematic process of getting ready for war. X wouldn't stop coming for me, and I wasn't sitting around waiting for him to take me out. I would finish this, while my powers were strong.

CHAPTER 22

Poseidon

I paced back and forth in my temporary home, trying to find something to keep me busy. The ocean's pull was almost impossible to ignore today. I tasted the salt on my tongue, felt the wind on my skin. Touched the scales of my Hippocamps under my fingertips. Why was I still on Earth when I was missing out on the life I'd created for myself in my palace under the sea?

I was here for Elyse.

When I closed my eyes, I sensed her soft skin under my hands. Her gasps and breathing in my ears. Her floral scent lingered in my nose and in my mind, the arch of her cupid's bow, the place her neck curved to run into her shoulder, the feel of her lips on mine.

That was what I stayed for. The human girl who'd

made me realize I needed to pause and do something for myself instead of preventing everyone else's lives from falling to pieces.

"Poseidon," Heracles said, appearing in front of me out of thin air. "Uncle."

"Heracles," I said, holding out my hand. Heracles clapped his hand into mine. He was smiling, but his eyes were tight around the edges.

"What's wrong?" I asked.

Heracles hesitated, his gaze dipping at first before meeting mine.

"It's Elyse."

"What happened?" My stomach bunched into a fist of nerves. If it was Elyse, whatever was wrong wasn't something small. Nothing half-assed ever happened to her. It was spectacular, and it was terrifying. Especially if Heracles was coming to me.

"She killed herself."

My ears started ringing. "What?"

"X went to her to finish her, and with her injuries, she didn't believe she stood a chance to beat him. So, she took control of the situation. But she's back. I mean, it's not her final death." His attempt at a half-grin came out clumsy and awkward.

"No, I know that," I said, still feeling as if I were going to vomit. "She did this to herself? Was it to get more power?" I doubted it had anything to do with being depressed, because she'd have known killing herself wouldn't be final.

He nodded. "She's looking for more strength. To get to X."

I shook my head. None of this made sense.

"But if she died—"

"She can't control it," Heracles finished my sentence. "She's strong, Poseidon. Stronger than I ever thought she'd be so quickly. But it's volatile power right now. Her magic isn't stable, and she doesn't know this. Won't listen to reason. And she's not going to sit back and wait until we can figure out what she can do."

"She's going to fight," I stated, realizing what Heracles was saying.

"And she might not manage," he said, nodding. "I think she might be out there right now. You know how fucking stubborn she can get."

Why was this happening? Why couldn't we just have one day of peace before everything blew up again?

"This thing with X... it's not my fight."

"Yeah," I said. I knew Heracles wasn't going to join in on this fight. I'd known it from the start. He'd had his day with Hades. And getting involved in family feuds that stole your soul more than once in an everlasting life wasn't fair.

"I need you to help her," he begged.

"Of course."

He nodded. "Maybe I need to speak to my father again and see if he's willing to lift this ban off me that's making it so I can't fight alongside Elyse, because in all honesty, it's killing me to sit back and do nothing." His voice croaked, and that time, his emotions showed themselves. "Okay, gotta go." He walked away.

There was nothing else to do at this moment. I couldn't hang around here; he'd warned me. And Elyse was the only priority. I marched into my bedroom and changed out of the semi-formal clothes I'd been wearing since I arrived on Earth and dressed in battle clothes. Leather pants because they didn't pinch, and they stretched when I needed to kick. A muscle tee because if there were no sleeves it meant easy movement. Shitkicker boots because I was going to kick some ass.

And I strapped every weapon I owned to my body. Knives and swords and throwing stars, a chain, nunchakus. When I was done, the metal rattled as I walked. I caught a glimpse of myself in the mirror. I hadn't looked like this in the longest time.

There had been wars, once upon a time. There had been days when I'd dressed like this all the time and fought side by side with the other gods, doing what needed to be done. Battling to win.

Those days were long gone, but I got a taste of the thrill, of the danger of what it meant to fight for something.

This time, there was an underlying fear that clutched at me. This wasn't about the humans, a war for their lives, the fights I did best. This was about Elyse and whether she was going to manage this fight at all.

I'd never been this worried about anyone. I'd fallen for this woman and I wasn't sure how this had happened.

I needed backup. So, I went to the one person who'd been sent here to stick by Elyse's side. I found Ares in a park.

"What the fuck are you doing here?" he asked when he saw me, his eyes narrowing in my direction, scanning me head to toe. "And why are you dressed like you're going to war?"

"Elyse is out to get X. She's stronger, but she has no control over her ability. We have to get this mess sorted, because if she gets herself killed another time, she's on her last life."

"What?" Ares asked, sitting forward on the wooden bench in the park. "She died again? How?"

I sighed a heavy exhale, and with Ares not saying anything, he must have understood what it meant when I said she was stronger, and he wasn't a fool to not be able to guess what she had done. "Herc said her power is out of this world."

Ares shrugged. "Is she all right?"

"Yeah, for now. So, come and help, Ares. Don't be a dick about this. It's Elyse we're talking about."

"Yeah, I know. And I know you have a thing for her. Who doesn't, right? She's the human girl all the gods go gaga over. But that's not my problem. I'm not a part of this."

I shook my head. "You sound like a real prick when

you talk like that, you know that?"

Ares chuckled. "You haven't called me that before. Nice that you're expanding your vocabulary."

"Goddammit, Ares. If you actually stand up for something once in a while, you might find that you have direction."

"Nice," Ares said. He sat back in his bench looking bored as fuck. "You should use that motivational speech when you recruit the other guys who are head over heels for her. Apollo might fall for it."

"Fuck!" I cried out, frustration building. "Don't you care?"

When he didn't respond, I shook my head. I wasn't going to waste my time here. I was about to leave when I said one last thing.

"If she dies and you did nothing, her blood is on your hands."

I left before Ares could say anything. Whatever cocky remark he had lined up, I was sure I didn't want to hear it.

On my way to Apollo, a shockwave rocked through me. The magic was strong and dark; it tasted bitter at the back of my throat. This was it. X was fighting. And if this much energy pulsed through the air and he wasn't right next to me, it wasn't about the humans but Elyse.

She was already there, and the battle had started. There wasn't time to recruit anyone else to help me. Elyse would be forceful after dying again, but she wouldn't have any control. Especially if it was so much more than Heracles had thought it would be. Elyse didn't stand a chance.

What the hell had she been thinking?

I didn't go to get Apollo or Hades or even implore Heracles to join the fight. I headed straight for Doom Central, the middle of the darkness that seemed to spread through Chicago like a plague.

As soon as the waves hit me, it was hard to breathe, and the darkness was cloying and sticky, like syrup from hell.

The closer I got to X and Elyse, the harder it became to see clearly. The power that shifted the very atmosphere around me was so intense, I wasn't sure which way to go and suddenly I was lost in a sea of magic that fucked me over so badly, I couldn't get to Elyse.

I tried to push it away with my power, bring rain that showered across the city with a cadence of its own. Energy bubbled over my flesh as I grew on the electricity. Thunder rumbled overhead, and I hoped the magic storm would let X show his face. But I was still lost, wandering around as if I were a human, not a god.

"Elyse? Where are you?" I called out. No response, and my stomach hardened at the idea I wouldn't find her in time.

After what felt like forever, running in circles, chasing my own tail, I ran into Apollo. He was drenched, but as soon as he stepped closer to me, my magic enveloped him as well and he was out of the rain. His blond hair clung in strings to his cheeks and he looked as ready for war as I was in black leather.

"What's going on?" he shouted.

"Three guesses," I said, gasping for breath as I scanned the area for any sign.

"I can't find them." His voice was strained.

He already knew what she'd done.

"This magic is ridiculous," I called out over the thunder and the rain that surrounded us. "X shouldn't be this indestructible. He should never have been this fierce."

"He went on a killing spree. The more souls he eats—"

"The stronger he gets," I finished, and Apollo nodded with a grim face. He stared around us and cried out, "Elyse!"

Nothing.

"Don't you want to do something about this darkness?" I growled. He was the god of sunlight or some such shit.

"I tried," Apollo said. "But this magic is fucking insane, and I'll admit, I'm not who I used to be."

I shook my head. "No matter. We'll find them."

Apollo nodded, and we headed out together. I wasn't sure we'd find them, though. And while we hurried, Apollo looked as nervous as I felt. He cared for Elyse. He had to. Who wouldn't? Ares had made that comment about all the other guys being interested in her. I hadn't wanted to believe it, but what else was there? I knew it. I'd always known it, somehow.

It wasn't just Hades. It was never just Hades.

We could work it out later. We had to get to her and make sure she wasn't eaten alive by X or something of the sort. We had to be sure she was safe.

And for that, we had to find her.

We searched for a while longer. The darkness was thick like fog now. When I breathed, it went deep into my lungs. I was a god, so it did nothing to me, but it could kill a human who inhaled it.

"Ares," Apollo yelled, and I looked up. Ares had joined us. He was dressed in leather, too, weapons hanging off him. He looked fierce, his green eyes glowing. He hadn't appeared ready for war like this in a long time, either. Even though fighting kept this guy going.

"Change your mind?" I asked.

"Are you kidding me?" Ares said. "This magic shit going on in the air is so strong, it's interfering with my signal. We need to kick this guy's ass so I can watch the movie I started when I went back home."

Apollo and I glanced at each other, and I rolled my eyes. Ares was such a fucking child. But he was here, and we could do with any help we could get. Maybe if we were all together, helping Elyse wouldn't be all we did.

Maybe we could actually stop this shitstorm.

CHAPTER 23

Elyse

X was stronger than when I'd last fought him. That hadn't been the plan. I was more powerful, and he should have at least remained the same. But I'd been out for five days. Or something like that—how long had it been again? In that time, he could have done so much damage.

And he had, by the number of news reports on missing people in the city.

Part of me regretted what I'd done when X confronted me in my bedroom, but I'd had no choice and had been otherwise screwed. I might not have had this much strength before, yet maybe Heracles was right that I should have engaged X to call the gods to me. What if they hadn't come in time? That, to me, was a risk too high to take. Still, if I had, I might have survived, and perhaps I'd have been able to slow X down, if not stop him so those who'd died over the last five days didn't all have to lose their lives. Just thinking of those innocent souls made my heart hurt because I was supposed to have saved them. However, I hadn't.

X was so powerful now it was, as if he'd inhaled an entire stadium of humans. It wasn't impossible he'd done exactly that, but the notion left me trembling that he'd soon become unstoppable. And as much as I stood brave, fear trickled through me, tossing doubts about in my mind that I was in way over my head.

My only hope was the energy that hummed through my veins. I could almost hear the vibrations like an electric current. I was on a whole new level. I'd be able to throw magic at X. Absorb it, too. I didn't know how I knew. But I did, as if part of my mind had unlocked secrets it'd previously kept from me. It had to be linked to being reborn.

"X!" I shouted when I finally made my way through the chokingly thick darkness. The city drowned in blackness. I didn't know where the humans were, but it was supposed to be daylight. Were they freaking out? I would.

I'd left my place at sunrise. But the heaviness that'd settled over Chicago replicated the dead of night, with no stars in sight. A blackout that swallowed the Earth.

"You don't give up, do you?" X growled in my ear, and I spun around. He wasn't next to me. He wasn't anywhere I could see, but my skin rippled with shivers.

When he laughed, the sound bounced around, echoing as if I were in the middle of the cacophony. X was everywhere. The night around me wasn't just a byproduct of him being here, it was him.

"This ends now," I called out, sounding a lot more confident than I felt. Point for me. I could still do this.

"You have a lot of power," X hissed, followed by whispers dancing on the wind.

"I'm glad you've noticed." I smirked. "It's all for you."

"It won't be enough," he declared, and the words echoed, swirling around me, boxing me in.

A tightness closed in around me, leaving me claustrophobic in this darkness with the sound of his voice wrapping around me, tying me up. "I have a lot more energy now, too." Mirth shadowed the tone of his words, and I pictured him grinning.

I didn't want to contemplate how he'd gotten his hands on it all. It was hard to think that Hades was somehow behind all of this. I struggled to believe it, in all honesty. He was full of shit, but this energy was X alone. Nothing about Hades felt like this.

Our intimacy was different—his energy tasted rejuvenating after I'd slept with him. X's was the opposite.

"Come on, girl," X said. His voice rose above a whisper and the sound scraped over my skin. "What do you have?"

I reached deep down and gripped this new power of mine, pulling it up, bringing it into the light. Or into the dark, rather. The moment I hurled my energy out there, the ripples of electricity spun out of control. It whipped me around like cords, pulling me up from the Earth and into the air, then slamming me back down as if my magic had a will of its own. As if it was acting out.

The air was knocked out of my lungs when I hit the ground, my whole-body aching, and X laughed.

"You're overeager, Elyse," he said. "But do it again. That was fun to watch."

I was furious, lava pouring through my veins. I wasn't going to lose this because I was fighting my own magic. I controlled it.

So, I drew my knife from the sheath on my back. It wasn't very flashy, but I'd fought with the weapon the longest, and it was my go-to. The moment I closed both hands on the handle, my magic charged into the blade and it shimmered with electricity, turning golden, throwing off waves of magic. I lifted it over my head, but it flew backward and dragged me along with it. I hit a building with my back and the wall split, the crack running up to the top and splintering pieces of rock onto me. The slicing agony along my back left me grimacing with pain, but nowhere near how much it should have hurt.

X barked his laughter again. "You're pathetic."

It annoyed the hell out of me. This wasn't good. The fight had only just started, and I was already losing. I hadn't even engaged yet.

X was suddenly right in front of me, his black body

materializing out of the night. He kneeled before me where I sat against the wall, leaning an elbow on his knee in a human posture. His eyes glowed with blue fire and his mouth opened all the way to his ears so the gaping hole was like something in a horror movie. He exposed his sharp teeth, just as black as the rest of him, even though he never used them. He breathed in everything he destroyed, all the life force he could find.

That didn't mean that he couldn't bite me.

"Come on, little one," X snarled. "Don't tell me you've given up. We're just getting started."

My knife was still lodged in the building at my back. But if the momentum was anything to go by, I could use that to my advantage. I yanked the weapon positioned over my head down and hurled it forward, aiming for X's brow.

The sharp tip hit home, and X's head split open. He let out a cry that cut me all the way to the bone. It was like nails on a blackboard, but so much worse.

He melted around the knife, his body falling apart, my blade slipping to the ground. I shuddered, unable to look away.

Was it this easy?

When he dissipated into the murkiness around me, I couldn't believe the outcome. It seemed too good to be true. This was too easy. But I wasn't foolish enough to believe him gone.

I scanned the street on either side of me, waiting for him to materialize. Waiting for something, anything. I was almost ready to believe I'd won, that my new power had actually saved my ass and gotten rid of X, when I became aware of two blue flames in the distance near a parked car. That was what I'd thought they were at first. They floated around on the road and after a while, I realized that they weren't flames but orbs. No. In fact, they were X's eyes.

Still alive, still burning. Fucking ass. They floated toward me, closer and closer. And I was hooked, staring into them, unable to tear away my gaze. X chuckled again, loud and coming from all around me. The laugh didn't just dance on my skin, it pushed into my mouth as I screamed, filling me up from the inside, clawing at my organs, scratching me the way he'd done to my arm.

And still, those flames came closer until it seemed as if they were inside me. And I was falling, falling, falling.

The next thing I knew, my dad stood in front of me. Tall, broad-shouldered, and wearing that long-collared shirt he'd loved. He smiled. The sun shone down on me as never before. The grass around us was greener, and I inhaled the scent of sea water from somewhere nearby.

"Dad?" My voice quivered, and I was unsure if it was really him.

He nodded, his eyes smiling as they always did when he looked at me, as if nothing in the world could make him stop loving me. "I've missed you, sweetie. Look how strong you are."

I took in a sharp breath, and my throat thickened. After he died, I'd daydreamed of seeing him again and again, finding out he hadn't actually been killed and had come back into my life.

Except now, I struggled to believe it was him. Why was he here? Around me was just a vibrant park flooded in sunshine. Birds sang in the trees, and a light breeze swept past. Why was I not back in Chicago? But right now, I didn't care. My dad was in front of me, and I'd cried so many nights, prayed to the gods for the chance to see him again.

I stumbled forward on wobbly legs, blinded by tears. For so long, my heart had been missing an integral part after I lost my father. My family. And now, seeing him again, the months of grief I'd faced came at me in waves, crashing into me, overwhelming me, strangling me.

"Dad!" I choked the word out. My breaths rushed as I tried to make sense of what was happening.

"I don't have much time, so listen carefully, baby girl. You're so strong, more so than any other Lowe before you."

"But I don't know what I'm doing." I wiped my wet cheeks with my fingers. "I'm in over my head." I moved closer to him, but he kept being just out of reach. I hurried to him, but he was always too far to hold on to. The grass softened under my feet, and I found I was barefoot and wore a white dress that flowed in the cool wind.

My dad shook his head. "Nonsense. You're doing everything you're supposed to. You're fighting, you're winning. You're loving. Have no regrets for the decisions you've made."

I shook my head. "Is that all there is to this?"

"Of course, sweetie. That's how all this started. With a whole lot of loving."

"What do you mean?" I asked, taking another step forward and another to him. My dad wasn't walking, but I could never get to him, and my hands tingled with the urgency to be in his arms, feel his strong arms around me, tell me everything would be all right. That I wasn't losing my mind or my humanity.

"How do any of us come into existence? You know how it works, don't you? You're a big girl now." He folded his arms across his chest, his short chestnut hair blowing in the breeze.

I tried to figure out what he was saying, but as I thought about it, darkness started to creep in from the edges around us. Not a lot at first—hardly noticeable when I'd grown up in a world where it had been an everyday thing. But the grass under my feet died. It turned from green and soft to brown and spiky. Clouds drew in so the sunshine disappeared and my dad wasn't smiling anymore.

"What's happening?" I asked.

"What are you talking about?" he asked, his eyes growing dull.

The absence of light crept in closer, growing thicker

and thicker. My dad frowned now, fear crawling over his face.

"Dad!" I called out.

He moved farther and farther away from me, as if he floated on air.

X came out of nowhere, taking form out of the darkness. Dad's eyes were glued to him.

"Don't look into his eyes!" I shouted.

But my father was riveted. He stared at X like a child and opened his mouth when X touched his chin. X glanced at me, his eyes laughing as he started to breathe in. Dad's life force spilled out of him.

"No!" I shouted, running to my father.

But I still remained in one place, despite my pulse racing. I searched for my weapons, but the dress offered nothing I could use. I kept running and screaming to get to my dad, to fight X, to stop him from taking my dad's soul.

But there was nothing I could do as I kept running. I watched in horror as he sucked my dad's life dry and the body turned into ash on the wind. I fell to my knees. Every breath expelled out of me, tears spilling, my heart breaking over and over. I sobbed into my hands, loud and hard. I felt barren, a shear of nothingness that threatened to shred my soul to dust.

With my scream, everything shattered. I was suddenly kneeling on the ground in the city again, wearing my fighting clothes, that blade still in my hand. It had all been a horrific nightmare, and the emotions still pummeled my chest. X had rolled my mind. And he had given me the worst terror I could have imagined. But it couldn't real. My dad, all my family members, were safe. Their souls were being honored as the souls of heroes by the gods.

It had just been a bad dream, or vision, or whatever the fuck it was.

X laughed, and I gagged at the sound. The noise bounced around inside my head.

"Did you think you could stop me?" X chortled.

I shook my head, tears still welling in my eyes, my heart bleeding from the vision of my dad. I climbed to my feet.

X was suddenly in front of me again.

"Don't overestimate yourself, Elyse. You're just a human. A mortal. You can't help it. When your lives are up, that will be it for you."

"It's not over yet," I yelled in his face, but I didn't sound as angry as I wanted to. The dream had unsettled me. I wasn't in control of my powers and I wasn't mastering my emotions, either.

"No, you're right." X stood so still, he might be mistaken for a shadow. "But until it is, I'll leave you with a little souvenir. A reminder that it will be."

His face was so close to mine, I squeezed my eyes shut, so I knew he wouldn't make me look into them again.

A sharp pain shot into my arm, and I cried out. X's teeth were lodged in my arm so deep that those black fangs scraped the bone. And from his mouth, darkness spread.

I lifted the sword and struck him on the neck. The power echoed through me like I was a tuning fork, but X let go with a squeal and disappeared. Suddenly, the night dissipated.

"Elyse!" Poseidon cried out and three gods—Ares, Poseidon, and Apollo—ran to me.

They'd been looking for me. My chest beamed with an overwhelming joy to see them together, coming to my side. An ecstatic sensation shoved aside the earlier doubts, because for the first time in ages, I didn't feel so alone.

"I see him," Apollo bellowed.

"Come on," Ares growled, setting after something I couldn't see.

"Take care of her," Apollo said. "We'll go after him."

Ares and Apollo ran away, disappearing between the buildings. I sagged against the wall, wondering how the hell I'd gotten out of this alive.

CHAPTER 24

Poseidon

She looked like death warmed over. And it wasn't because she'd killed herself, either. X had pulled her through the wringer—easy to see that. The stench of putrid death clung to her clothes and her hair, and when she looked at me, dark circles swam underneath her eyes, as if she hadn't slept in months.

"Are you okay?" I asked, kneeling in front of her.

Elyse grabbed on to my arms, clutching at me, terrified. She was trembling, and her shoulders shook as she started to cry.

"I think he killed my dad," she said in a raspy whisper.

"X?"

She nodded against my shoulder. "I just saw him do it now."

God, what the fuck was Hades playing at, giving X this much freedom? Did he know it was getting out of hand? Did he care?

"It was a nightmare, Elyse. It wasn't real." I drew her into my arms as her body trembled.

"It felt real. And I couldn't stop him." She sniffled and it killed me to hear the agony in her voice.

"He's gone now. You stopped him well enough that he left."

She broke away and glanced at me with eyes filled with pure terror. I hadn't seen this in her before. She carried herself as a warrior, stood up against anything, never backed down. But this time, she was a sliver of herself, deflated and hurting. It worried me to see her in this state.

"He'll be back. But I want to know, why did X send the Aeternae creatures after my dad in the first place, with so many of them ambushing him? Was he targeting my father?"

"I don't know." The truth was all I could offer.

She was right. This wasn't over. Apollo and Ares were attempting to stop X from killing more innocents. But Elyse didn't have to worry about that with us around anymore. I touched her cheek, cupping her face with my hand.

"It's going to be okay," I reassured her, looking into her red-rimmed eyes. "It'll be fine. We'll deal with this, okay?"

She nodded and took a deep breath, letting it out with a shudder. "My magic is too strong," she admitted.

I kneeled where she sat, glancing up at the building, at the crack that ran up the length of the tower. "Did you do this?"

She nodded and lifted the sword. "With this."

It was just an ordinary blade. The damage she'd done with it was close to what the gods could do. This wasn't just power that had doubled when she'd died. It'd become exponential. And that didn't make sense at all. What had Zeus done when he'd given them his power? What had his goal been? Elyse was different from the other Lowes. It was almost as if now that there was only one left, she had the power they should all have shared. All pent up in one body.

But that didn't make sense.

"Come," I said. "We should get out of here."

"Will the others be back?" She stared down the street in the direction they had left.

I didn't want to share her with Apollo or anyone else right now. I just wanted to give her comfort and remind her she was safe and protected. I didn't intend to wait, either.

I nodded and stood, helping her up by an elbow. She cradled her arm, and I frowned, releasing a long exhale. I touched her wrist, and she lifted her arm, looking down. Bite marks lined her skin, deep wounds that looked awful. But the wound didn't worry me. The skin had gone black around the injury as if the flesh was rotting.

"What did he do to you?" I asked, my heart beating so fast, my voice shook when it shouldn't have.

"He bit me," she said softly, studying the mark.

I shook my head. I'd never seen anything like this. What the hell was going on here?

"Elyse." I sighed. "You can't keep doing this."

"Doing what?" she asked.

"You have to stop going after him."

She frowned. "Are you telling me what to do?"

"Yes," I said. "This is madness. You can't do this; you're not strong enough. He's become something even I don't understand."

"I will continue to go after him," Elyse said tightly. "I just need to train and harness my power. Imagine if I use the Dragon Punch with this power. Or any of the other weapons I've trained with. X won't stand a chance."

"No, Elyse. You're done," I ordered, staring down at her.

I didn't want to see her hurt. She'd been through so much the last couple of days, it was a miracle she was still in one piece. But that wasn't the half of it. That black wound bothered me. What if he'd marked her somehow, or injected a piece of himself inside of her? What if this was how X would defeat her, suck her in after all?

I was terrified that something would go wrong, and there was so much about X we didn't understand.

"I'm not done, Poseidon," Elyse retorted. She took a step back, still cradling her arm, but her power rippled over me as her anger grew. She was more powerful than she realized, and it was out of control. That was a problem.

"If you don't stop, he'll kill you," I said, trying to be reasonable.

"And if I stop? He'll kill all the humans. Is that okay? I'd rather die."

I saw red. Elyse might have been willing to sacrifice herself, but I wasn't going to make an offering out of her. I wasn't willing to lose her now that I had found her. Was it selfish? Absolutely. But when had I ever been selfish? I cared about this—I cared about her.

"Look, let's just get you home," I said, attempting to keep my voice down, to hold my anger in check. "We can talk about what all this means when you're patched up and well-rested. Let's forget about saving the world for a moment."

Elyse shook her head. "No, Poseidon, I'm not just leaving the humans to fend for themselves. I was put on this Earth to do what I am doing now. My dad didn't lose his life so I can give up. It's my destiny. I know you want me safe, but you don't get to tell me what to do. You might be able to boss your brothers around, but you are not here to do the same with me."

I huffed loudly. That was it, the last thing that pushed me over the edge. "Do you think this is what I do for fun?" I shouted. I was acting out, losing my temper when I shouldn't have. But Elyse had hit a nerve. "Do you think looking after my brothers is what I wanted to do with my life? Trust me, being a babysitter twenty-four seven for the rest of my immortal life wasn't exactly the future I'd envisioned for myself. But look at you, look at what you've done to yourself!"

"And? What about it?" Elyse asked, raising her voice to match mine. "At least I'm doing something about X. Between the gods and me, you guys are stronger. But it fell to me to stop X—only Zeus knows why—and so far, until now, it looked like I was the only one getting up to face this asshole. It seemed like I was the only one who cared about humankind."

I couldn't believe we were fighting, screaming at each other when a moment ago, she'd fallen apart against me. Couldn't we go back in time to when she'd needed me?

"Don't tell me how I feel about the humans," I snapped. "I have been ruling over them for a lot longer than you have been alive. Centuries, millennia, eons. Caring about the humans is the whole point."

"Yeah? Well, you have a shitty way of showing it." Her glare shot daggers my way.

And maybe she was right. Maybe the gods hadn't shown how much they cared for the humans in a long time. The proof was right in front of us—X running rampant, and we hadn't really done a hell of a lot about it. But then again, X was Hades's problem and he'd let him get out of hand. For the first time, I was worried about myself, caring about my own happiness and Elyse was the one human I was interested in. For a change, I wasn't running around after everyone else. I was doing something for me.

Did that mean I was shirking my responsibilities? I hated to think that it was true. I was the most responsible god there was. But that meant I could be responsible for my own life, too.

Elyse cleared her throat. "I like what's happening between us and adore where this is going. But I'm not in this so you can tell me what to do. I'm not with you because I need someone to guide me. Somehow, I thought we could be equals." She laughed bitterly. "I guess I was delusional, thinking I could ever be equal to a god."

I shook my head. I was scared of losing her—I'd come so close so many times. I cared for her more than I'd ever cared for anyone and it scared me I'd fallen for her so fast. What if I lost her? Where would that leave me? An eternity was such a long time to spend alone—I'd been there. But Elyse had mistaken my affection for dominance. And maybe it *could* be mistaken for that. I didn't know anything else. And she was fighting me every step of the way.

"Fine," I finally said. "If you want to ruin your life and kill yourself, I can't tell you what to do. I wish you'd stop and think for a moment, but I know it's out of my control."

"Damn right it is," Elyse replied, her voice clipped. "I can look after myself."

A response fluttered at the forefront of my mind, but I bit my tongue. Anything I said would only make it worse. We needed to stop and take a step back, calm down, reevaluate. We were talking past each other, and it only looked to her like I wanted to change who she was. That was the farthest thing from the truth.

If I had intentions of making a go of something between us, I had to pull back and work with her. She wasn't like the gods who needed orders, she was independent and strong and some of the many reasons I was drawn to her. And I had no intention of losing her, so I'd do whatever I needed to show her I would respect her wishes. Of course, it went against my better judgment, but I'd have more influence if I was in her life rather than pushed aside.

So instead of retaliating yet again, I turned and walked away. Nothing I said now would come out right. I was leaving so it didn't get worse. I hated leaving Elyse behind when she had battle wounds, when I yearned for nothing more than to take care of her and make sure she was okay.

But if she was so serious about being in control of her own life, I had to let her do her own thing. It ripped me apart to walk away, but it was the best thing to do if it meant she didn't think I was telling her what to do.

The intensity with which I cared for Elyse burned through me. I had no idea how to deal with what had happened—X hurt her in a way he'd never harmed anyone before and I didn't know what the blackness on her skin meant. Was she infused with darkness now? Would it spread until it killed her and she died for good, taken by X?

I didn't want to go home and worry about her, struggling with my thoughts. I didn't want to go to my palace, either. It didn't matter where I was now, it would be lonely. I'd drive myself crazy thinking over everything that had happened.

Mount Olympus was out, too. The last thing I needed was to have to put on a face in front of all the other gods.

So, I went to the only place I knew I could just be me. It was ironic, but I ignored that.

Hades was home when I marched through his front door. He looked up at me from his position on the couch. Was this all he ever did? Watched movies and played games?

"What are you doing?" Hades asked when I collapsed on the other couch.

"I don't know if you care," I said, "but X is really becoming a problem, and I worry Elyse isn't okay. But there's nothing I can do about it when she pushes me away."

"You too, huh?" He stared me up and down.

I glanced at him. What exactly had happened

between him and Elyse? I'd never asked. From early on, I'd understood he was in love with her, but I'd never questioned why they weren't together. After all, Hades had proven he was capable of love in some way with Persephone and how he'd fought to keep her. Sure, it had been a spell, but his devotion was to be envied, and I refused to believe such passion was solely from the curse. It had come from him.

But I wasn't sure I could unpack all of this now. Instead, I turned my attention to the television. "What are you watching?"

"Reality TV," Hades said. "It's fucking hilarious. It's all about the humans and the petty shit they get up to. I can't believe they put this on as entertainment. We should get these channels back on Mount Olympus. Maybe I'll run the cable down to the Underworld."

I laughed. Not because it was funny, necessarily. But because if I didn't laugh, I'd cry. But right now, I knew exactly what I had to do to help Elyse.

CHAPTER 25

Elyse

When I wasn't in a fight with X, and I went about my daily business, there was no sign I was stronger than I had been before. The power that had run through my veins when I woke up after dying was gone. The electric current that charged me on the way to the fight hadn't returned in a couple of days, and I was starting to wonder if it had been a one-time thing.

Aside from a few scrapes and bruises and the awful bite on my arm, everything had returned to normal. My body healed fast.

The darkness that had shrouded Chicago disappeared as if it had never been. There had been no more news bulletins of people disappearing. It was as if X had retreated completely.

But I wasn't fooled. Maybe I'd have believed it if I didn't have a constant reminder of the death I'd been through twice. This time, it wasn't only the dark that came back to haunt me from time to time that told me X wasn't gone yet. My arm hurt like a bitch and not just because X had chewed through my flesh straight to the bone. Fifteen stitches later, I'd lied on my medical records that I had been attacked by a large dog. The nurse that patched me up hadn't believed me by her blank stare when I explained what had happened. But she hadn't been able to find any other excuse for the holes in my arm and insisted on a Rabies shot.

Nothing else made sense in the human world.

But it was the black night that spread across my skin that was the real reminder this wasn't over. The nurse had tried to scrub the darkness around the wound clean, thinking it was dirt. The pain had been so excruciating, and I'd held back the cry in my throat until she gave up. No matter how much soap or other disinfectant they used, the dark patches wouldn't disappear. She called the doctor and her advice was to take antibiotics and referred me to a specialist. Except, this was something else X had done to me.

Every time I changed the dressing, I studied the blackness, trying to decide if it was growing or not. It was my biggest fear that it would consume me, and I'd go under without X even being near me. Or maybe this was him being near me—maybe this was him being a part of me now. Marking me.

Whenever I thought about it for too long, I broke out in a cold sweat and my body trembled. I had to consciously change my mind to avoid any panic attacks.

I hadn't spent any time with the gods in the past few days. After my fight with Poseidon, he'd disappeared, too. Or maybe he hadn't—I hadn't exactly made the time to find him. Or anyone. I needed alone time to ground myself, let everything I'd been through sink in. Find myself because I'd been running nonstop, and for my own sanity, I craved solitude.

Apollo had checked in on me once or twice quickly, but I hadn't known what to say. I didn't have any problems with him, but I was scared and embarrassed about what I'd done. How I'd reacted. Sure, I'd saved myself, but the idea of taking my life sat heavily on my shoulders. Especially after seeing how the gods in my world had reacted, the fear etched on their faces, the disappointment in their voices.

Apollo didn't try to tell me I was wrong—bless him—but he didn't have to. I knew I'd fucked up when there were other options, like fighting X until the gods arrived.

As for Ares, I assumed he was around town on his own, causing shit wherever he felt like it and not committing to anything in particular. It seemed like the thing he did, and I couldn't blame him. It seemed all the gods weren't ready to return to Mount Olympus... Sure, Zeus had instructed Ares to join me, and let's be honest, I hadn't exactly been welcoming. Maybe I'd give him a real chance to get to know him, see what he had to offer to assist me against X.

And, of course, there was no sign of Hades. Why would he come to me? I hadn't seen him since our fight at the training center. Maybe he felt bad for knocking me out. I wasn't a fool and knew he'd taken me home and tended to my injuries before vanishing.

Sometimes I wondered if everything with X was Hades's last hurrah. He was laughing all the while because I'd lost, and I couldn't shake this damn darkness that followed me around like a stray dog, waiting to nip me on the heel. But on the other hand, I struggled to believe he would consciously do this. I couldn't work him out.

Someone knocked on my door, and I frowned. Apollo usually just arrived. Since I'd killed myself, I hadn't seen Oliver—Heracles had scraped his memories of those days, but I was sure he wanted nothing to do with me. Which was just as well. I had no idea how to deal with him if he came on to me again.

Other than that, I had no idea who could be looking me up.

When I opened the door, Catina stood there. She looked unsure, her eyes like a small kitten needing my help, as if I'd maybe tell her to go away. Except I'd never been happier to see anyone in my life.

"You have no idea how much I need you right now," I said.

Catina's eyes glistened as if she might cry. "I thought you'd tell me to get lost."

I shook my head. "I'm done being a bitch. Seriously, I need to learn that other people are right, too."

Catina shook her head and hugged me. I winced when she brushed against my arm.

"What's wrong? What happened?" she asked when she saw my bandaged arm. When she glanced at me, her face had changed. It was acceptance. "Training injury."

I nodded. Maybe she knew I was lying. If she did, she'd accepted it. If she didn't, she believed she knew me well enough, and that was perfect. She was the only person who was a real friend to me right now.

It wasn't that Heracles wasn't my friend, but since everything had gone south, he'd kept himself busy with his classes. I hadn't even trained with him. I think we all needed a bit of time to wrap our minds around what had happened, to come to terms with how things had turned out.

And maybe I was hoping he'd take the time he had away from me to find a way to forgive me.

"Can I offer you coffee?" I asked.

Catina nodded and walked into my apartment behind me.

When we sat on my couch, each with a giant mug of coffee in a semblance of life before everything had gone wrong, Catina stared at me with concern. "Are you okay?"

I wanted to lie about my life and nod, but I was trying to turn over a new leaf. I was starting to learn I wasn't an island—I had to see the people, and gods, around me as friends, not enemies. They were all here to love me and take care of me.

So instead of lying about how I felt, I shook my head. "I can't even begin to explain to you what I've been through the last couple of days."

Catina looked down at the mug in her hands. "Something tells me that even if you do try to tell me, you'll leave a lot of it out."

I intended to defend myself, but Catina held up her hand to stop me. "And I don't blame you, either. I haven't made it easy for you to talk to me. And that was wrong. So, tell me about what's bothering you. No matter what it is, I promise I'll be open-minded about it and try to see it from your point of view. It's the least I can do as your friend."

I took a deep breath and let it out with a shudder. "How do I say this? I guess I am dating… Phil." I'd nearly said *Poseidon*. "But we're fighting right now."

"About Al?" Catina asked.

I shook my head. "No, they're all right with each other." At least, I thought they were. "We're fighting because I can't allow someone to take care of me, and Phil is a lot more caring than anyone I've been with before. I guess I push everyone away, even when I don't want to."

It wasn't exactly that simple, but it was the most

human way I could think of to describe what we were going through. It wasn't just about letting go and being vulnerable, though. Poseidon had a legitimate reason to be worried about my safety—killing myself had only been the beginning of my problems. I couldn't explain any of those things to Catina. At least I could talk to her a little, though.

"I guess I just don't want to be controlled," I continued. "I don't like being told what to do. Can I have love without that?" Those words seemed so heavy, as if I could spend weeks trying to unpack them and what meaning lay beneath them. Exactly how my life felt.

"Of course you can," Catina said. "Love is all about compromise, about someone accepting you for who you are."

"But that means I have to accept them for who they are, too, doesn't it? Phil can't be the only one to compromise."

Catina nodded, taking a sip. "Unfortunately, that's how it works. But if the love is good enough, pure enough, that won't matter in the long run."

Maybe she was right. It felt great to get advice from someone who was so down-to-earth. I'd missed my best friend and these talks. Could I risk the rest of this conversation?

"These guys aren't the only two," I started carefully, eyeing her for a response.

Catina raised her eyebrows, but she didn't get upset with me the way I thought she might.

"There are more?" she asked.

"I had a fling with one of them. I think I told you about that. But there is another guy, too. Nothing happened between us." If the playful kissing and almost-sex with Ares was *nothing*. "But his don't-care attitude really gets me. I think I'm attracted to him, even when I don't want to be."

"How do these guys feel about you?" Catina asked, her posture soft and relaxed as she sat back in the couch, unlike the last time we chatted about this topic. Her smile encouraged me to open up.

I straightened my shoulders and released a long exhale. "I guess there's an attraction. But I have no idea if this can go anywhere. The thing is, they're not just going to walk out of my life anytime soon. Which means I have to figure out how I'm going to deal with this."

Catina just sipped her coffee, thinking about my response in silence.

"Look, I don't know the full situation," she finally said. "So I can't give you the best advice. But I can tell you that as long as you follow your heart and do what you feel is right, everything will fall into place."

I smiled at my friend because she was right. Heracles had said something similar, about not fighting what I felt for the men. "That's the best advice you've given me in a while." And I meant it. I was relieved I could turn to her about this. It was great that we were friends again.

Catina laughed. "To be fair, it's the first time we've spoken in a while. So anything I said to you right now would have been a great suggestion."

I was about to answer when there was another knock on my door. When I opened it, Oliver stood in front of me.

"I hope I'm not intruding," he said, peering over my shoulder at Catina. "I don't know what's going on, but you've been on my mind for a while now. Are you okay? I just feel like I had to ask you that. Don't know why, but there it is."

I nodded and opened the door wider. "Why don't you join us? Catina and I were just catching up."

Oliver smiled, as if he'd expected me to reject him. I wasn't sure how much he still sensed of the trauma I'd put him through or how much he did and didn't remember. But being surrounded by humans, talking and laughing about nothing much and having coffee seemed like exactly the kind of thing I needed right now.

Oliver sat next to Catina, the two of them breaking into small talk while I made another cup of coffee. When I walked back to the living room, the three of us sat together and joked around, talking about trivial things.

And I had to admit, it felt great just to be normal and do human things for a change. It was calming not to have anything to do with the gods.

CHAPTER 26

Elyse

A week or two passed with no sign of X. I searched for him, but came up empty. My life carried on as usual. I woke up in the mornings and went for a run before I trained with Heracles, learning how to control my new power.

The first couple of sessions with Heracles had been awkward. He was still angry with me for taking my fate into my own hands and doing something as crazy as killing myself. He had different views on how to approach this whole thing with X and the way my power was growing. But I'd started to learn not everyone did things the same way, and if I was going to be myself, I had to accept some people wouldn't agree.

After a few days, Heracles had accepted what was happening and we fell back into a rhythm. We were back to being friends, even though there was nothing to discuss that really mattered.

X seemed to lie low. I hadn't seen him for a while, hadn't heard any news about people disappearing. And the wound on my arm had healed—the stitches had come out and I didn't have to bandage it up anymore. Even though the darkness hadn't disappeared and my skin was still tainted, the blackness didn't grow. I was starting to get used to it—like an ugly tattoo.

Now and then, Apollo came to see me. It was great hanging out with him—we talked about things, getting to know more about each other, and I realized he was quite a sap. He loved poetry and music, even though he was shy about discussing them. He even started writing me love notes, which I adored and kept in a wooden box in my bedside table. And whenever he was with me, my life seemed just a little brighter. He was my ray of sunshine.

Sometimes we didn't talk. We made love. Some nights we spent the darkest hours between the sheets, exploring each other's bodies, getting to know each other in a way that words would never describe. Other times, he took me to various places around the world, spoiled me with gifts and chocolate. He was worried about the mottled darkness on my arm, but since it wasn't growing and there was nothing we could do to make it go away, we left it.

My relationship with Poseidon was a little strained since our argument. Even though my feelings for him were still strong, it was as if the two of us struggled to find a stride. We were almost too careful around each other—he didn't want me to think he was controlling me and I didn't want him to think I felt trapped.

He took me back for another chariot ride, and that day, I laughed more than I'd done in so long as we raced dolphins. Poseidon had a softer side to him, and he cared so much. Still, the days I didn't see him, I missed him and I counted down the hours until I could be with him again. To find a way to make us closer, to get to know him on a deeper level, to show him how I felt, I was trying to be understanding.

Unsurprisingly, dividing my love between two men wasn't difficult at all. I'd thought dating two different guys would be challenging, that I wouldn't know how to split my heart. But it seemed like the easiest thing in the world. Like Heracles had said, the gods loved deeply but not exclusively. And it seemed I was a lot more like them than I realized before.

After I trained with Heracles, he was off to meet up with someone, but he refused to tell me who. Part of me contemplated following him, but I wasn't sure I was ready to cross this path after what we'd just gone through, so we parted ways. I set out into the city to take photos for my portfolios, for Tina at *Foundation* magazine and other projects. I worked with *Foundation* the most compared to my other freelance clients. Probably thanks to Catina, who always put in a good word for me.

The days I spent with her at the office were easily my favorite. It felt as if I were connecting with my human side again, and Catina was proof of that. Even though I tried not to spend too much time with Oliver, I saw him now and then, too. Just to strengthen that connection.

On Wednesday afternoon on the third week after everything had happened, I emerged out of the *Foundation* offices into the fresh afternoon air. Lately, the sun showed its face more and more often. It felt like it correlated with how well Apollo and I were doing, but that was probably a coincidence.

I stepped off the curb to cross the road to my car when something grabbed me around the throat and yanked me backward so fast I couldn't breathe. Panic soared through me. I hadn't been on my guard—everything had been so normal I'd stopped expecting attacks. I was pressed into a corner between two buildings, and I struggled to breathe with something wrapped tightly around my neck.

Darkness filled the space around me, as if I drowned in blackness. I clawed at my neck, a scream pressing on the back of my throat. Sweat drenched my skin, my pounding heart thumping in my chest. Fear churned in my gut, knocking all sense aside, replaced by the dread of this being the moment I lost my battle against X.

His face pressed up right against mine, those fiery

blue eyes terrifying to look at. I still had nightmares about the blue orbs floating in the darkness.

"I've been waiting to get you alone," he hissed.

His hand wrapped around my throat, the fingers digging into my skin, nails piercing my skin. A paralyzing hurt spread through me as I couldn't dislodge him and kicking him wasn't helping.

"That's enough," a voice bellowed behind X.

He craned his neck around to look over his shoulder. Ares stood right behind him. He was tall and muscular, his hair cut almost right against his skull and those green eyes fierce. He was dressed for battle—metal armor clanked when he moved. I cheered on the inside at seeing him. Best sight ever.

"Let her go," he barked.

The Ares who stood before me now looked nothing like the sullen, sulking god I'd seen before. He exuded confidence and authority.

X laughed and turned away from me, but his fingers were still wrapped around my throat. I felt my power jolt inside me, but I worried if I let the energy loose, I wouldn't be able to control the ability. It was so much more than it had ever been before—I hadn't nearly had enough sessions with Heracles to prepare me for this. I admitted that now, knew I'd been too gung-ho before.

"Do you think you're enough to stand up against me?" X asked, his voice filled with hate.

This was where I was going to die. Had I lost my nerve? Been knocked down to size and realized how strong this monster really was? Whatever I had to thank for this dose of reality, I knew between Ares and me, we couldn't take him.

"He might not be able to do it alone, but he's not alone," Poseidon said, appearing next to Ares.

I wanted to scream with delight.

"Oh, look, you've brought a friend. How quaint." X was a sarcastic little bitch. It didn't suit him.

"Friends. Plural." Apollo stepped forward, dressed in the same leather and weapons as the rest of them. Neither Poseidon nor Apollo wore armor like Ares's, but they didn't have to. They were fierce, and the three of them together looked like they would be able to do some damage.

"I stopped the three of you before," X hissed.

"But you've never had to go up against all of us," Hades said, joining the rest of them. With the four together, they were a thick wall of muscle and leather, and if I weren't so terrified, it would have been a massive turn-on. Despite everything that had happened recently, I was no fool and understood I had four men in my life, four guys who affected me like no other, four gods who had turned my world upside down. And they weren't going anywhere.

I'd never seen the four of them together, and I had no idea how to react to any of it aside from staring in awe.

X let go of me abruptly, and I fell to the ground. I rubbed my neck where he'd gripped me. That was definitely going to bruise. I'd need a mirror to know if the skin had gone black, too.

"Why don't you just leave her alone?" Poseidon asked.

"This isn't the end of it," X said. Before any of us could respond, he disappeared as if he'd been nothing more than a figment of my imagination.

"Well, that was easy," Hades said.

"Only because he made it easy," Poseidon said. "You have no idea what he is capable of. Or what he has planned next. But we know he wants Elyse."

"Yeah, he does." Ares didn't look impressed. "This is his mess, remember?" He glanced at Hades, who rolled his eyes.

"I came to help, to be part of a team. But if this is what it's going to be like being here with you guys, I'm out." He ghosted away before anyone could say anything.

"Well, that didn't last long," Apollo said.

I knew Hades was pissed at how they were reacting. And maybe later, I'd try to find out what was upsetting him. Try to patch things up, because I was tired of the arguments, the drama. If we were to defeat X, we had to work as a team. But right now, I had to deal with the fact that two of my lovers were standing side by side and Ares was here too, and he didn't seem to mind.

"I'll go get Hades," Poseidon said with a sigh. "I'll see you soon, Elyse."

Poseidon disappeared, too.

Ares looked at Apollo. "Well, if that isn't the way it always is, I don't know."

"Let them figure it out. We don't want to get between the brothers." Apollo looked back at me. "Are you okay?" he asked. He lifted his hand and tentatively touched my neck.

I nodded. "It's going to bruise. Is it… Is it black?"

Apollo shook his head. I sighed in relief. At least that was one good thing.

"Listen, I have to get going. I have something to take care of for Heracles." Apollo pressed his lips against mine briefly. "But I'll be back and then you and I are going on a date."

I had so many questions, but when he brushed his thumb across my lower lip, I melted against him before he disappeared, too. Catching myself, I glanced around to find just Ares and me.

"Phew!" he exclaimed. "That's a bit too much heat for my liking."

I laughed. Ares was such a comic relief when everything got too strained. That was when he wasn't on his own mission, ranting and raving about how unfair life was. Something I hoped he could learn to get over, so he could just enjoy the other gods' company.

"Thanks for coming," I said.

Our last conversation had been strained, but Ares had been here. They all had been. And it meant the world to me.

"Sure," Ares said. "It's what I'm here for, right? Zeus

would kill me if he thought I was neglecting my duty of watching over you." He winked, offering me a cocky grin, and I smiled, shaking my head.

Ares took a step closer to me, and we were nearly pressed up against each other. Despite the metal between us, my body warmed up. I might have said *no* to Ares before, but that didn't mean I wasn't attracted to him. The sexual tension between us climbed until it was noticeable.

"Of course, just because Zeus sent me doesn't mean it's the only reason why I'm watching you."

He leaned in as if he were going to kiss me. My breath caught in my throat and I closed my eyes, but before his lips made contact with mine, he vanished, too.

Well, this disappearing act was getting old fast.

ABOUT MILA YOUNG

Mila Young tackles everything with the zeal and bravado of the fairytale heroes she grew up reading about. She slays monsters, real and imaginary, like there's no tomorrow. By day she rocks a keyboard as a marketing extraordinaire. At night she battles with her might pen-sword, creating fairytale retellings, and sexy ever after tales. In her spare time, she loves pretending she's a mighty warrior, walks on the beach with her dogs, cuddling up with her cats, and devouring every fantasy tale she can get her pinkies on.

Ready to read more from Mila Young? Subscribe to her newsletter for latest updates and new releases: www.subscribepage.com/milayoung

For more information...
milayoungauthor@gmail.com

42242462R00177

Made in the USA
Lexington, KY
15 June 2019